CHANGES IN
CRYSTAL SPRINGS

JENNIFER LOUISE HAES

CHANGES IN
CRYSTAL SPRINGS

TATE PUBLISHING
AND ENTERPRISES, LLC

Published by Tate Publishing & Enterprises, LLC
127 E. Trade Center Terrace | Mustang, Oklahoma 73064 USA
1.888.361.9473 | www.tatepublishing.com

Tate Publishing is committed to excellence in the publishing industry. The company reflects the philosophy established by the founders, based on Psalm 68:11,
"The Lord gave the word and great was the company of those who published it."

Book design copyright © 2014 by Tate Publishing, LLC. All rights reserved.
Cover design by Gian Philipp Rufin
Interior design by Jake Muelle

Published in the United States of America

ISBN: 978-1-63122-661-8
1. Fiction / General
2. Fiction / Family Life
14.02.28

For my father

CHAPTER ONE

This Christmas, I got a penknife in my stockin' and was pretty disappointed considerin' I already had one, the blades not dull and all. But Stepdaddy showed me a tiny pair of scissors that slid outta the side, and I considered that mighty fine. Mama never let me have scissors 'cept the baby kind with round edges, and this here pair has point enough to poke your eyes out.

Stepdaddy gave me a wink over the rim of his coffee cup, and Mama just sighed and gave over.

First, I cut up little things like wrappin' paper and ribbons and just a few threads offa the carpet. I held off on other things later. Like maybe Felicity's hair. Maybe while she's sleepin'. I couldn't help it; I looked at her and grinned.

"What?" she said as she saw me. Her eyes narrowed, 'coz she don't trust me none. So I just say "Nothin'." And go back to my stockin'.

Felicity is my sister and reckons she has to live up to her name, which she says is "elegant." That's sposed to be somethin' really special, I reckon. She wears makeup and earrings and sometimes calls us others common.

Mama's just 'bout had it with her, and Mama's been sayin' that for a mighty long time, so I reckon it takes too long to had it for my taste. 'Sides, Mama says if her name's so elegant, she was the one that picked out that name when Felicity was borned, and Mama shouldn't hafta to pay for it now. And since Mama picked out that name, she can change it too, so Felicity better mend her ways afore she becomes a Plain Jane.

I swear Felicity spends near all her time fussin' with her looks. She irons her hair to make it smooth. She says she hates her nose and she hates her hair and she hates her eyes. To my way of thinkin', if she can smell and see, well, why worry? I think she looks fine the way she is. 'Course I don't tell her that 'coz she's my sister. But her eyes are big and brown and all her lashes are long and so black they look like spider legs. She's all arms and legs right now. Mama says she'll grow into them in time. I hope so, 'coz right now she's always trippin' over things or knocking things over. Felicity is gonna be a lot taller than Mama, and skinnier, too. Mama's kinda small and kinda plump and her face is so sweet you just wanna crawl into her lap for a hug.

Me and Mama and Felicity and Stepdaddy live in the old trailer park in Crystal Springs. I dunno why they call it a park. I mean, there ain't no swings or fountains or flowers. Anyways, this Christmas, we got us a tree, 'coz we have Stepdaddy livin' with us. We put it up the week afore Christmas, and I helped hang the bright gold garland and all. Stepdaddy called me his "little man," and Felicity done made those sounds like a horse sneezin' or somethin' when he said that which to my way of thinkin' ain't too elegant if you ask me.

After we turned on the tree, the 'lectricity in the trailer flickered a little bit. This here tree takes up a lot of space, and the livin' room weren't that big to begin with. But Mama and me, we like the fresh smell that this kinda tree makes and Mama says it'll last a long time, even when the tree is throwed out 'coz the Minnesota winter will freeze the smell right here in the air.

'Sides my knife, I got warm green mittens, a soft orange, some nuts, and candy in my stockin'. Last night, we opened the real presents, and I gotta new game, marbles, and colorin' books. I hafta say I weren't too pleased with the colorin' books. The pictures were baby-like, you know, bunnies and stuff like that. I kinda hid 'em aside when Mama weren't lookin'. I didn't get no new crayons. She said my box of old crayons will do for a while, even though the black is pretty wored down.

After presents last night, we sang some songs 'bout Baby Jesus and all and ate supper. We had a big chicken this year that Stepdaddy bought with his Christmas bonus. Mama roasted it and even made mashed potatoes for me, 'coz they's my favorite. Felicity complained 'bout the mess they make, but we all ignored her. She didn't wanna get her new dress messy. She was wearin' it 'coz she was goin' to midnight mass with her best friend, Mary Ellen. Seems to me like I'm always too young to go to midnight mass. Seems to me like I'll never get to walk in the dark and the snow and see the church lit up with candles and all. Mama says next year, but mamas always tell you that you'll get to do stuff you want to do now next year. Seems to me, though, they always ferget. Folks always like to remind you that you ain't big enough to do what you really want.

Mama got all excited like she does on Christmas Eve and put out Christmas cookies and little bit of a glass of milk by the stove pipe. She said I had to go to bed early for Santa Claus to come. I didn't have no heart to tell her that I knew there weren't no Santa Claus. Jimmy Henderson, my best friend at school, done told me that couple weeks ago at recess. After I punched him, I decided what he said made a lot of sense. See here, this here Santa is the only person you ever did hear of who went alla way round the world. And he knows everyone; he visits 'em in one night. He's awful old to do that. Now Granddaddy can't barely make it down to the barn and back, and he's younger than this here Santa. 'Sides all that, no one has seen Santa, and he wears this here bright red suit of velvet with big black boots. You'd reckon someone would notice him sometime. Don't know why I ever believed that to begin with.

When Jimmy came round to ask could I go sleddin', I knew we was friends even though I punched him, and he said he was gonna get me back. Jimmy's been my best friend ever since we moved to Minnesota from Tennessee two years ago. He lives in a proper house and not one made outta tin and his windows don't hafta be cranked open with the handles fallin' off all the time. I hate our windows. Can't even see outta 'em 'coz they have glass slat things that ain't even clear glass.

I like Jimmy's house. It has a big old yard with a tire swing and a slide. And inside, he has his own room with lotsa toys and games. They have a color television too and a car. Goin' to Jimmy's house is like goin' to a fun park. I only been a few times, though. Jimmy's mama is a nervous kinda person what always stares at you funny. Even though she calls me "dear," I can tell she don't mean it none. You can tell when a person is usin' a real smile or not. You can tell if they really mean what they say. See here, when you talk to someone, you kinda like to look 'em in the face. That's why grownups always tell you "Look at me when I'm talkin' to you." But Jimmy's mama, she looks round the room and out the windows, everywhere 'cept your face. Folks reckon you can't see that if you're a kid. But sometimes, I can tell a person better'n Mama.

Anyway, after our stockins' Christmas morning, Mama made oatmeal and put raisins to mine 'coz it's an occasion. We're goin' to 10:30 mass to talk to God for a while, and then Christmas is over for another year. Seems to me it sure goes by fast considerin' how long it takes to get here.

Father John is sayin' mass today, and I like that 'coz Father John smiles a lot and talks 'bout funny stories just when you start to get bored. He's real smart that way. Mama says when I'm older, I can help serve at mass. I don't tell her I don't wanna do that. Those boys wear funny dresses and hafta learn Latin, and I have a hard enough time keepin' English straight. I ain't ready for no foreign talkin' yet. Someone done told me

I would be takin' Latin classes in a few years time. I sure do hope they was just razzin' me.

Stepdaddy ain't goin' to mass today 'coz he had to work real hard last night. He says he's goin' to take a nap and that'll make his holiday. I remember when Mama made me take naps. Sure ain't my idea of a holiday, not at all. Seems to me since he's a grownup and can do anythin' he wants to, he'd pick another way to have a holiday. Grownups sure don't know when they have it easy.

Mama helped me put on my tie and coat and new mittens. She looks real pretty in her dark green dress, and we walked out into the cold, cold air. The hairs in my nostrils stick to the sides of my nose, so I try to breath through my mouth. But that makes my teeth hurt somethin' awful. Mama always holds her head up and walks proud through the park. She says we're way 'bove any meanness round us. Now, the ground looks pretty level to me. There ain't many hills round these parts anyhow. And our neighbor, Widder Kaine, gave me cookies yesterday afternoon, which ain't so mean, but I agree with Mama 'coz she likes me to.

We walk to church, which seems a lot farther than usual when it's this cold. We stamp the snow from out boots outdoors afore we go in. It wouldn't do to stamp your feet inside, 'coz God won't be able to hear everyone prayin' to him. Walking by the holy water, I remind myself to give it a miss on the way out, 'coz I know how cold it'll be.

We always sit in the back and kneel to talk to God first thing. Mama's always got a lotta things to say, but

I stay put and squeeze my eyes real tight and wait for Mama's sigh to tell me she's done. I don't have much to say to God anyhow, 'coz I haven't knowed Him that long. God was here long afore my granddaddy's granddaddy. That's so long ago it gives me a headache just to try and picture it. Seems to me, God coulda hung round a lot longer: I sure woulda liked to meet Him and talk to Him face to face. Course Mama says I can talk to Him just fine from here, but it's hard to talk to someone if you don't even know what they look like. So I sit back in the pew and enjoy the music and incense and all. We come every week, but Christmas is best 'coz Jesus was borned. Easter Sunday is good, but it's a really scary time afore that, Him being nailed and all.

Finally, the church people start comin' down the aisle. They's got their really fancy Christmas robes on. Father John has his head bowed a little and I see his lips move as he prays. Father John was borned in a place he calls County Cork way across the ocean in Ireland. That's why he's hard to understand sometimes when he talks. Father is a short man with frizzy white hair and blue eyes. His eyebrows go this way and that and look so bristly I figger they must itch an awful lot. He is most always smilin' and happy. You always feel safe when you're with Father John.

After Father John has thanked us for visitin' the church, we get to go downstairs for coffee. I drink cocoa and munch a doughnut, but outta the corner of my eye, I see Sister Mary Margaret, and I get real nervous 'coz the day afore vacation began, she done took my slangshot away. I reckon she's gonna tell Mama; her smile don't fool me none. Then Father John comes over, and he puts his hand on my shoulder. His hand is big and comfortable and fits just fine.

"Ah, here be my little man, and sure you be having a blessed Christmas."

"Yes, Father, I am."

Father John don't ever ask questions, and it sure makes it easy to talk to him. Sometimes, you don't hafta say nothin' yourself at all, and you still always walk away feelin' real happy and kinda smart.

Mama and Father John are talkin' in real low voices, and since I can't hear nothin' I keep eating my doughnut. Sure enough, Sister Mary Margaret is standin' next to me. She is short and chubby and looks real jolly, but like Mama says, looks deceive. She wears thick glasses that make her blue eyes so big I swear they can look all round me. And through me, too. Jimmy calls her Sister M&M, but I don't 'coz I know she'd know, and that'd be that.

She gives Mama a Christmas hug and smiles real big 'n' all. Course Mama asks 'bout my schoolwork, and Sister says I'm doin' real good with rithmatic and readin' but gotta work harder on my grammar and diction. Then they both look kinda serious at me. The doughnut don't wanna go down my throat. I feel sorta like I'm standin' between two generals in an army and both of 'em are wonderin' whether I should be sent to the front lines or not. That's where all the fightin' is, the front lines. I seen a lot of war movies, so I know all 'bout generals and front lines and such. I know the front line is 'bout the worse place you can get sent to.

Worser than the Mother Superior's office. I mean, you can get shot dead at the front line. Mother Superior just gets out her ruler. So I try to look like I don't care too much. Anyway, you know Sister Mary Margaret has more medals 'coz she works for God and all and what she says goes. Even Father John mumbles somethin' and walks away. I sure feel lonely when his hand leaves my shoulder.

Then Sister turns to me and says, "Robert was very active in school before we broke for the Blessed Holidays."

That sure makes me come to alert. Mama too. Folks are leavin' the church basement. Everyone is happy and the emptier the church gets, the more Sister's voice echoes.

"What are you planning on doing during your vacation, Robert?"

I tell her I'm gonna read and stuff like that. It's what Mama likes to hear, and I reckon Sister would be happy 'bout that.

"I was wondering," Sister says, as she's lookin' in my eyes and then at Mama. "We need help over at the school painting some trim. Surely, Robert wouldn't mind spending a few hours helping us."

I been holdin' my breath so long, I feel dizzy.

"Well, Bib?" Mama is askin' me but not really askin', if you know what I mean. 'Coz she knows I know I gotta do what Sister says. Mama's got smooth dark hair and gentle brown eyes that can smile all by theirselves. Those eyes ain't smilin' now. Her lips may be smilin', but not her eyes. She's looking right deep inside me and there's a little warnin' light in 'em to remind me to be polite and to obey.

"Yes, Sister." My breath comes out in one big whoosh.

"Good. I'll see you Wednesday morning at 8:00." And she nods her head. I reckon she's happy 'coz she's won.

When we're left alone, Mama looks at me a while then nods too. She rinses her cup, zips me up, takes my hand, and we go back out into the cold.

Though I probably got off easy, I'm still mad that I only have one sure day of freedom left.

The wind's picked up some, and the old storm door slams against the outside wall when we go into the trailer. Inside is real warm and smells all piney and spicy with good wood smells comin' from the stove. I take off my boots and put 'em on the newspaper by the door just like I'm told. My shoes are wet, so I take 'em off too and go into the livin' room. Stepdaddy and Mama talk a little, and then Mama says why don't I go to my room and play my new game called Operation and needs lots of practice. I go, but I know they's getting' me outta the room, so they can talk 'bout what Mama and Father John were whispering 'bout.

I'm only eight, but I reckon I can tell when somethin's goin' on or not. Grownups like to tell you what you know and what you don't know, but us kids know a lot more'n grownups think we do. Somethin's been goin' on in this here town for a long time. Grownups used to smile more, but now, they talk in groups all closed up and talk and stare. Even the playground looks like

Main Street what with kids standin' round whisperin' and such.

Me and Felicity share a room in the back of the trailer, far enough away from anythin' bein' said in the livin' room. One side is mine, and one side is hers. There's a striped Indian blanket hung between. She's lyin' on her bed, and the smell of the new nail polish she got in her stockin' is real bad. I start to crank the window some, but she yells at me to stop. She's fifteen, and I gotta do what she says, but I hate that. One of her smelly hands moves the blanket.

"What are they talking about in there?"

"Dunno."

"Well, what did they say to you when you left the room?"

"Mama said to practice my game."

"Heaven's sake, Mother doesn't care about your stupid game. Didn't you hear anything?"

"No." The cellophane on the box comes off real hard. I go to my burro for the batteries 'coz they's not included.

The blanket stays open, and Felicity watches me. She sure wants to know somethin' and if I know what she wants to know, I sure ain't tellin' her.

Finally, she asks, "Was it about me?"

I just shrug and try to match the plus signs and the minus signs in the little box.

"Give it here." Felicity takes it from me and puts the batteries in. One side of the black battery box gets smeared with red nail polish, but I don't say nothin'. I open the little bag of white pieces which are really neat. There's a wishbone and a little pencil and a heart and other stuff. You put 'em in the proper places in his body. This is how you play: you get to be a doctor and operate on this man with a real surprised look on his face. You do that with metal tweezers. But you can't touch the sides of the little openin's when you operate 'coz that wakes the man up, and his nose flashes red, and there's a buzzin' noise. He already looks real scared, so you don't wanna do that.

Felicity pulls the blanket along the rope a little more. Then she sits and watches me. Sometimes, I feel like we're all waitin' for somethin' to happen. I just don't know what it is.

CHAPTER TWO

Tuesday mornin' started out all cloudy and gray, but the sun came up while I was eatin' my cereal, and I watched it brighten up more on the icicles and then bounce off all over the place outdoors. There's one big icicle growin' long the front of the trailer, and when it gets real big, I'm gonna break it off and suck the point all down.

I check but Mama put the sugar bowl outta my reach, so I just take another bite of toast.

Mama and Stepdaddy are drinkin' black coffee and starin' out the window. They don't talk much in the mornin', and I don't know why. Just stare a lot. I used to reckon there was somethin' real interestin' outdoors, and I'd look and look. But never did find anythin' even movin' usually. I like mornin' myself just fine. But I learned not to talk to 'em. They try to answer, but their eyes look like they ain't focused. Now I leave 'em alone.

Along the row of trailers, I can hear our neighbor Miss Alice's big yellow dog bark for his breakfast. His name is Cannon Weight. Felicity calls him a mutt, but Miss Alice and me, we say he has "mixed heritage."

Miss Alice taught me that, and I reckon it sounds fine. I decide I'm gonna visit Miss Alice after breakfast and afore I go sleddin' with Jimmy.

Usually, the radio's on while we eat breakfast, but Mama said the news this mornin' is too ugly to listen to. That means there's a lot of news 'bout this here war going on in a place called Nam. Lots of folks get killed there, you see, and that makes for sadness, and Stepdaddy says sadness ruins our digestion.

I think a lot on this here war in Nam. Stepdaddy showed me where Nam is on a little globe he keeps. It's so far away, I asked him why we was fightin' there. He just sighed and said, "Son, I don't think anyone even knows anymore." Now that don't make a lick of sense to me. At school, when some kids are fightin', it might get bad some. But the next day, those kids don't fight no more. Seems to me our soldiers should do the same thing, and everybody can come home. That's what these here protestors say, they say, "Bring our boys home," and if that's what folks want, I sure would reckon the generals and whatnot would listen. I mean, seems like this war started long afore I was even borned. Someone is awful mad, I reckon.

After I put my cereal bowl in the green sink, I start to put on my outdoors clothes. This takes some time, but I sure don't wanna catch my death. Boots take the most time, 'coz they hafta go over my shoes and both my shoes and boots are kinda small. I hafta sit down and put plastic bags over my shoes so the boots will fit. Then I have to buckle 'em. There's six buckles on each boot. It sure is tirin'. And the plastic bags make my feet feel hot and slippery.

"Where are you going, Bib?" asks Stepdaddy.

I tell him 'bout sleddin', and Miss Alice and all.

"Oh, that reminds me," says Mama, and she goes through all the piles of stuff on the small table next to the telephone. She comes up with a round tin of Christmas cookies with a big red bow stuck on.

"Give this to Miss Alice and wish her a Merry Christmas from all of us, and thank her for the brownies she left at the door yesterday."

"Mama, Christmas was yesterday."

"Well, tell her anyway and remember your manners."

Manners is somethin' grownups are real big on. Sometimes more than schoolin'.

Miss Alice's trailer is bigger than ours and sits between Old Mr. Johnson's silver trailer and a little bit of woods. It's the only trailer in this here park that's painted. It's called "Robin's Egg Blue," and that's true 'coz Jimmy and I once found a piece of robin's egg last spring and that egg was 'zactly the color of her trailer. She's got the biggest yard too, and a whole big section in back where she plants tomatoes and such. She put a mesh fence all round the garden to keep Cannon Weight out. Now you know Cannon Weight is big enough to crash through that there fence if he wanted to. But he sits and looks at it with his head to the side restin' on his shoulder. Miss Alice and me, we know Cannon Weight is the smartest dog in the whole world, 'coz even though he could get into that garden, he don't.

But he does run through the cornfield that runs behind her trailer. He likes to hide and let me find him.

Miss Alice owns her trailer and her yard, both. She don't rent like the rest of us. Once she showed me her deed, and it was real thrillin' to see to my way of thinkin'. It's a government type of fancy paper. And it's full of big words we had to look up in the dictionary. Course after we looked up one word, we'd ferget the meanin' when we read the next sentence and had to look it up again. But that don't really matter, 'coz it's the fancy printin' that counts, and the big signin's at the bottom.

I stomp the snow offa my boots on her top step and knock at the door. I like the tinkle of the little bells that are attached to the door window, but I don't knock again 'coz it would be impolite.

Miss Alice is always happy to see me, she says. She's 'bout my favoritist person in the world. I dunno how old she is; somewhere between an older aunty and a younger grandma. Most times I stay a long time and listen to her stories 'bout her nieces and nephews and the other folks in her family. I feel like I know 'em real well 'coz she points at their pictures long the shelf on the wall in her livin' room when she talks 'bout 'em. I like her stories a whole lot, and we laugh all the time. She moves her hands when she talks so's they look like little birds a-twitterin'.

I never been able to figger Miss Alice out. All the neighbors call her a shocker 'coz she wears a long straight black hair wig and lots of makeup and big fake jewels round her neck, wrists, and in her ears. She never wears mama clothes, and her trailer is full of smells like perfume and incense, which covers the smells of her animals just fine. If other people start to do what they call gossip about her, Mama says Miss Alice has a big heart and that shuts other people up most times.

Miss Alice was never a mama, and that makes her real sad 'coz now she's too old. Old Mr. Johnson says that doesn't keep her away from men though. Now, I once told Mama this at the supper table, and she got real mad and done told me to hush. That there was the first time I decided to tell somethin' I heard but didn't understand. To my way of thinkin', it was a good plan, 'coz Mama or Stepdaddy would give a clue as to what Old Mr. Johnson said. But I reckoned wrong.

Miss Alice always has cookies or fresh bananas and oranges for me to eat. She don't never have candy. Even at Halloween. She says how candy rots your teeth and all. Then she shows me how she can push all of her top teeth out with her tongue. I reckon she hopes that'll scare me, but boy, I reckon it's real neat, and I'd sure like to be able to do that. I don't tell her though 'coz she might never do it again.

Miss Alice loves Mama's cookies and pours me a glass of chocolate milk, and we eat 'em sittin' together at the kitchen table. She understands the troubles of puttin' on boots and never makes me take 'em off, even when they leave a long puddle under the table while I swing my legs. We talk 'bout Christmas and school, and she tells me lots of stuff 'bout her pets. I don't mention Sister Mary Margaret 'coz I have a feelin' Miss Alice would take Sister's side of things.

Two cats live in the trailer long with Miss Alice and Cannon Weight. One of the cats is a big orange one, with one and a half ears. He don't like most folks, but he likes me fine. Miss Alice says it means I'm a cat person. I like that. She says this here cat, Tom, has gone and lived five of his nine lives and was only two years old. Her other cat, Dill, well, he is the best cat ever. He's fluffy and gray striped and me and Miss Alice share him. Sometimes, Mama lets Dill come into our trailer to play and couple times he slept over in my bed. Right now, he's sittin' on my lap, and I rub his belly to make him purr.

I'm real sorry I can't stay to hear more 'bout Dill and all. But I tell Miss Alice I gotta meet Jimmy for sleddin'. She understands and afore I go, she tightens my scarf, so I can hardly breathe. I don't loosen it till I'm outta sight of her window. Then I start the long walk to Courage Hill.

Simon Peter, who's in me and Jimmy's class at school, called it Courage Hill after he done dared us all to go down it with our eyes blindfolded once. We froze a path that winds down round lots of trees and rocks, and we piled snow real high to make a jump. It took Simon Peter, Jimmy and me a long time to tote enough water to freeze that path. After we were done a lot of kids from school came to use it, which made us kinda mad 'coz they sure didn't help none in makin' it. Some kids are real afeared to go all the way down, so we show off slidin' down the length of it. Course we know where the pitfalls are.

Jimmy's all ready and waitin' at the end of my road and yells "Bib!" real loud and all excited 'coz he can't wait to show me the new sled he got for Christmas. It's made of plastic, so it really flies. My sled has metal runners that rust. I hafta wipe 'em dry at the end of every day I use it.

We trudge to the top of the hill and sit a while talkin' 'bout our presents and how awful it is to have sisters. Poor Jimmy, he's got three and no brothers. One of 'em calls me Gnat every time I go over his house and play. She makes fun of my name, but I don't say nothin' 'coz I have to watch my manners. I tell her my little cousin couldn't say "Robert" when she was little and called me "Bibber" instead. Then everyone started callin' me Bib. She just laughed at me. She's kinda rude to my way of thinkin'. Once, she put salt in my cocoa instead of sugar, but I drank it anyhow. I weren't gonna give her the satisfaction of sayin' nothin'. But it surely did taste somethin' awful, and I almost did throw up.

Jimmy goes first down the path, and I follow. Round the bend of the big oak, you gotta turn your runner left or you're a goner. He can't do it with the plastic sled and yells and turns over in a soft snow bank. I'm right behind, so I turn off too and land on my face. We laugh till it hurts and go to the top to start again.

After a long while, we stop and stay at the bottom of the hill. Jimmy sits down in the snow, and I sit next to him. His chin is in his hand and looks like he's studyin' on the lines of trees ahead of us.

"Bib," he says, "my mom says I can't play with you anymore."

I'm quiet 'coz it does feel like my stomach has flipped and my heart has stopped. I put my hand on the ground 'coz I'm spinnin' too.

"How come?" I ask, and I turn and look where he's lookin'.

"I dunno." Finally, he looks at me.

"Maybe she only meant for a little while," I said, and I'm hoping it's so. I know what mamas are like when you don't do your chores and such.

"No. She says not at all. She and my dad are real worried about something."

We're both of us real quiet. I dunno what Jimmy's thinkin', but I feel real small like I done somethin' bad, and I don't even know what it is I done.

"Jimmy, do you know what's goin' on round here?"

"Nope. But I have to do what my mom says. She knows I'm with you today, but she said it's the last time."

That sounded too final to even think on. Jimmy's miserable, and so am I. We sit together and don't say nothin' for a while, and then he gets up to go home. He's facin' the other way when he says "I gotta go. See you later."

"Yeah." I watch him as he makes tracks in the smooth snow toward town afore I turn round and follow the two sets of tracks we made comin' here. My sled feels heavier and heavier as I drag it along. I wouldn't mind just leavin' it along the road 'coz I never wanna use it again.

I know I'm too big to cry, but I do, and the tears freeze on my cheeks and can't go no further than my chin.

CHAPTER THREE

Mornin' comes, and I don't wanna get up, not at all. I most always wake up early and like it, but not today. I roll over and put my head under my pillow and pull up the counterpane. When I was little, I used to suck on the nobly parts that make a pattern, but I don't do that no more. For some reason, I do feel like doin' it now. I ain't no baby, and I wonder why. I guess it's 'coz I'm just all sad. All I can think of is my day with Sister Mary Margaret and no Jimmy to complain to.

Stepdaddy opens the door and comes over to my bed. He sits down, and his arm goes round my waist, and he gives me a hug. This makes me wanna cry just like yesterday. I surely hope it's not gonna become a habit. I'd be teased an awful lot at school if it does, and I sure done been through enough of that when we first came here, 'specially when kids found out my nickname was Bib.

"Time to get up, Bib." He's quiet so's not to wake Felicity snoring on the other side of the blanket though she don't believe she does. "What's wrong?"

"Nothin'."

"Yes, something is bothering you. Come on, son. You know you can tell me anything. Imagine me as your friend."

"I thought Jimmy was my friend." I didn't mean to, but I done said it, and I feel just a little better even though I said it under the pillow. Stepdaddy heard me even so and pulled me round, lowerin' his head till our eyes are so close you can see how nice he is.

"Tell me about Jimmy."

"His mom won't let me play with me no more."

"Anymore."

"Yeah. And we don't know why. She won't say nothin'."

"I see." He takes a long time answerin' me. I heard a kinda sigh, but then he smiled.

"Sometimes," he says in that soft voice he used when he reads to me, "things are said or done that are mean and ugly, and the people who say them don't realize how much those words actually hurt us. We do this because of a thing called ignorance. You know what that means, son?"

"No."

"Well, now, ignorance is a terrible thing that people learn when they don't listen to their own common sense."

"I don't understand."

"You will understand, sometime soon too. But there is something just as important that you understand now."

"What's that?"

"That I love you, Bib. And I won't let anything or anybody hurt you."

This hug sure makes me feel better. And I ain't cryin' either, which is good.

After I dress, I go into the kitchen, and Mama's makin' pancakes. "It's the last of the flour." She laughs as she sees my face. "But payday isn't too far away."

We even have syrup, warmed up on the stove. I like to shred my pancakes into pieces afore I eat 'em. Then I pour more syrup on, and I think on my Stepdaddy.

His name is Sam Harper, and we met him three years ago down in Tennessee. Mama worked cleanin' our apartment house for rent and a little board in the city where we lived, what was called Florence. I asked Mama why it was called a lady's name, but she didn't know. Maybe 'coz it was named after a famous city in a place called Italy. So I asked why that city was named for a lady, and she didn't know that neither. Maybe Florence meant somethin' special in Italian. Then I asked what was Italian, and she said Italians are people in Italy. So I asked why we were called Americans and not English, but this time, she didn't answer and asked me to go find the aspirin.

Anyway, Sam Harper lived upstairs from us in a small room. It didn't hardly get no light 'coz the window faced the brick wall only some feet away. He used to say he got all the sunshine he needed when we visited us.

Stepdaddy has a real education. He was a school teacher in Florence. But he quit, and him and Mama got married, so we moved up north. I asked him once why he didn't teach no more, and he said he couldn't fill innocent minds with lies and still like hisself. I don't know what that means, but it made Mama real proud.

Now he works at the potato plant outside Crystal Springs, right outside the county line. When I first met Stepdaddy, I 'bout fell over in surprise. He's gotta be one of the most tallest men in the whole world. He's over six feet tall! Even though he's kinda skinny, he has wide shoulders. And when he really laughs hard, that whole thin body weaves back and forth like a reed inna wind. You only see his wrinkles when he laughs like that. He's kinda old. Thirty-two his last birthday. He don't have gray hair, though, like a lotta old men.

Mama's been real happy since she and Stepdaddy got married. They talk a lot 'bout stuff that's important and stuff they like. Sometimes they're not asleep till way after bedtime. They read books together on purpose. And he has a whole 'clection of records that he brang with him. Last year, a song came out called "Brown-Eyed Girl," and Stepdaddy says that song is 'bout Mama. Sometimes, he grabs somethin' to look like a microphone and sings it to her. When he gets to the part "sha la la la la la la la la ti da ti da," Felicity and me join in and dance round her.

Mama don't talk 'bout my real Daddy none. I guess she's still mad he up and died. My Aunty Selma, who's Daddy's sister, told me he was a no account, which I reckon from things I've heard on television has somethin' to do with numbers. I have a picture of him on my burro. He's not too tall, but he's standin' next to a big car with his foot on the fender. In his hand, he's got a flat bottle, and he's squintin' into the sun under his hat. He looks kinda mean even though he's smilin'. Looks like he'd rather punch you than say hi. I keep the picture anyway, and sometimes, well, afore Stepdaddy came, I'd talk to him. Just stuff 'bout school and all. Felicity laughed when I done this. She remembers Daddy and won't talk 'bout him even a little bit. Her face sorta freezed up if you even say his name, which is Bill.

Course breakfast can't last forever, and too soon, Mama is wrappin' me up in piles and piles of clothes. She says it's only ten degrees out, so I need extra protection. She tells me she's proud of me and to be good. I'm glad she's proud of me, but it's not like you can be anythin' but good when you're gonna spend the day with a nun.

I sorta slam the front door shut to let them know inside that I'm none too happy to be goin'. I walk as slow as I can and kick a piece of ice along the way. Once I slip and fall right on my back. It scared me some, but I moved my arms, then both my legs and reckon I didn't break nothin' so I'd have to keep goin'. I'm wearin' so many clothes I hafta kinda rock back and forth on my back until I can get on my side and heave myself up— first on my hands and knees, then all the way up. I like winter, but it sure can cause some problems.

Inside the school, it's none too warm. It's a big drafty cold building. I reckon the nuns don't feel it too much, 'coz they wear so many clothes, even over their heads and under their chins. When I pass the holy water, I give it a miss again, this time on what folks call principle.

I watch Sister for a bit at her desk. She's got a bunch of papers in front of her. She picks one up and frowns.

When Sister Mary Margaret frowns, her eyebrows come together over her nose. Papers that make her frown go in one pile, and papers that don't make her frown go in a banilla folder.

"Good morning, Robert." Her voice makes me jump 'coz I didn't see her lookin' at me.

There's a whole wall of what she calls Wayne Scottin' all the way round the room. It goes up from the ground to a little 'bove my chest. The color is real ugly, looks like old mustard dried on a picnic cloth. I always hated it but not enough to wanna paint it myself. Sister hands me some sandpaper and tells me how to rub nice and smooth so's the old paint comes off. Then she goes back to her desk. The only sound is the big clock tickin' on the wall. It's loud in the room, and I pretend it's music and sand on the off-beat.

A long, long time goes by, and I look and see I've only got maybe two inches done. My arm is achin' like anything. I know I'm gonna end my days here, sandin' off old mustard paint.

"Look, Robert," Sister says, and she's pointin' out the window. The window is next to her desk and I hafta go all way round the room to see, and I wonder if it's a trap. But she done give me the Sister look, so I have to go.

Outdoors, it's come on all bright and shiny, and the branches are coated with diamond ice. There's a bird shelf out there and the birds are fightin' over the seed that's spilled on it.

"Look at the chickadees. They can hang upside down from the shelf and still eat the seed I've put out for them."

I tell her chickadees are my most favoritist birds, and she tells me all kinds of things 'bout them. That each one hides seeds to eat later, and they can remember thousands of hidin' places. And when they's afeared, well, that's when you hear a lotta "dees" in their song. Of a sudden, a red squirrel shows up to eat some of the overflow. Both of us laugh at the squirrel, we can hear him squawkin' even through the window. Then I stop, 'coz somehow seein' Sister laugh surprises me and scares me at the same time.

Sister leans back in her chair and lifts her hand to take off her glasses. And Holy St. Patrick, I'm so afeared that I squeeze my eyes shut as tight as I can. Jimmy done told me if she ever done that her face would melt off.

But she's callin' my name, and I know I hafta look at her, so I open 'em real slow, and she hasn't melted at all. Her face is just old and small and her eyes are normal small with lots of crinkly lines round them. She looks tired, like mornin' don't suit her none.

"Robert, you have learned in this very classroom that we, as Christians, value the sanctity of life in all God's creation."

"Yes'm."

Now she's openin' a drawer of her desk, the big one that has all the good stuff she takes from us kids. My slangshot comes out and lies on the desk lookin' awful big. I see that the rubber part is wored a bit.

Sister looks real sad as she says, "Robert, tell me truthfully. What were you going to do with this weapon?"

"Gosh, Sister, that ain't no weapon. That there is just for target shootin'. We line up cans on Mr. Alderson's fence, and we make them knock over and all."

"You do not use it to harm birds or other animals?"

"Course not. I'd never do that."

And then I tell her 'bout Miss Alice's animals and especially Dill and how we share him and all. Sister fiddles round with the slangshot and squints through the forked part.

"Do you wanna try it?"

"Want to, Robert."

"Well, Ma'am, I can learn you how."

"Robert. I am not aware that there is a word listed in any dictionary such as *wanna*."

"Oh. But do you wanna try it?"

And she laughs real loud, I dunno what at.

"Get along with you. Take this beastly thing with you."

"But the sandin'…"

"Oh, yes. The sanding. Well, I guess Mr. Jensen can take care of that. He is our caretaker. Now mind what I say."

"Yes, Sister."

"When you return from your vacation, I shall expect a one-hundred-word composition waiting on my desk, Robert. It shall be called 'The Beauty of God's Creation,' and here is a list of words that I do not wish to see used in your composition."

I look down on the paper she hands me. The words are printed in big letters, so's I don't make no mistakes.

HAFTA
SORTA
WANNA
AWFUL
REAL
SURE

"Yes, ma'am."

"I shall also expect an improvement on your diction. Practice your *—ing* endings. Regarding the word *don't*, please remember where it does and does not belong in a sentence. That means no double negatives, Robert. Now go along. I have a lot of work to do." She puts her glasses back on and waves me away to the door. For a bit, while we was standin' at her desk, I felt we were friends. Now she's just a teacher again. I'm real relieved, 'coz I sure have enough complications right now and all.

Seems like the walk home takes a lot less time than gettin' here. When I turn into the dirt road you follow to the trailer park, I see an old pickup truck parked but runnin'. The exhaust from the pipe in the back flows out like lots of little clouds in a hurry. They's three men in the front, and they all have suits on and no coats. It sure looks funny to see 'em in an old pickup truck. They's lookin' down the road and holdin' up a map. I can hear 'em arguin', but I don't look at 'em real close, 'coz they might be strangers, and I can't talk to 'em.

I stop along my way and talk a little to Cannon Weight. His nose is big and cold, and he snuffs my pocket. When he sees I have nothin' for him, he walks away. Miss Alice's blinds are shut, so I guess she's takin' a nap. Old Mr. Johnson is puffin red in the face 'coz he's tryin' to dig out his Ford. Old Mr. Johnson goes to town every Wednesday, but nobody knows what he does there, 'coz he comes home late. He never has groceries with him or nothin'. That's what folks say, anyhow. I keep tryin' to stay awake so's I can hear his Ford when he comes home. But I most always falls asleep.

When he sees me, he throws his red shovel in the snow and straightens up. I can hear the crick in his back, and it must hurt 'coz he groans and puts his hands on his back like he's tryin' to hold it up. Old Mr. Johnson's hair is all white, and he's got big ears with bristly hair in them. That there hair must make his ears itch somethin' awful. I think he's least eighty, but Mama says he's still young, only sixty-somethin'.

"Well, Bib. A fine afternoon today. At least, the sun is warm."

"Yes, sir, Mr. Johnson. Want some help?"

He hands me the shovel, and right away, I scoop up too much snow, and I'm off balance. The snow's fallin' right back to where it came from. But Old Mr. Johnson doesn't say nothin' and I try again, a little snow this time. Now I'm really puttin' a dent in that snow bank. It's harder than I thought, balancin' the long wood handle and the wide red part, all at the same time. It's fun, though, and I sure don't understand why grownups complain about it so much.

While I shovel, I ask him 'bout the men in the pickup, if he knows 'em and all. He don't, but he gets excited, the grownup quiet kind of excited, and asks me lots of questions. But like Felicity always says, I don't know much.

Old Mr. Johnson shakes his head and mumbles somethin' 'bout trouble comin'. He remembers I'm there and thanks me for a job well done.

"You've done a real man's work, Bib, and you've done it well. I think you deserve this." He fishes in his pocket and brings out a nickel.

I'm dyin' for a nickel.

"But Mama won't like me to take money just for helpin'. Heck, Mr. Johnson, we're neighbors."

Old Mr. Johnson smiles and gives it to me anyway. I know we're both hopin' that Mama won't find out.

CHAPTER FOUR

I take my mitten off as I walked toward home so's I can feel the nickel in my pocket. First, it's as cold as the dyin' cold round me, but my fingers warm it up until it's just burnin' to be spent.

Mama's not spectin' me home, and I think on turnin' round to go uptown to the Five and Dime. But if Mama is lookin' out the window makin' beds or dustin', I know she'll see me. Last winter, she knitted me an embarrasin' green cap with a bright orange pom-pom on top. She told me when she knitted it that it would help her find me in a crowd. There ain't no crowds in Crystal Springs, so when she told me that I thought we was goin' to the cities. But no, she said we was stayin' right here. But still if Mama says she could find me in a crowd in the middle of St. Cloud or somewheres she can sure see me goin' down a dirt road that fronts eight trailers. So I go on home.

Soon, as you go up the steps, you can tell the stove's gone down. Hit's warmer inside than out, but not very. The cast-iron door on the stove has a handle that you hafta lift up and out. It gets real hot so Stepdaddy keeps an old oven mitt hangin' there. When I add a few sticks and a small log, the flames flicker a bit, then come alive again. I leave the door on the stove open awhile to warm myself. Felicity's on the sofa readin' a book. She's the one that let the stove run down.

"How come you're home so early? Mother said you wouldn't be back until noontime."

"Sister left me off."

Felicity shuts her book and looks on me like I'm crazy.

"Sister Mary Margaret?"

"Yep." Now my front's all warm, so I turn round and let my back catch up.

"Sister Mary Margaret let you off."

"Yep."

"I can't believe it. She never lets anyone off of anything. You had better be telling the truth, Bib, because if you didn't go, you're in big trouble."

"She said I could go."

"She probably got sick of your ugly face." She picked up her book again and ignored me.

"Where's Mama?"

"She said she had an appointment. She wore her good hat."

She's actin' like this is somethin' every day, Mama leavin' in the middle of the mornin' and wearin' her good hat and all. I can't believe this, so I go look for myself.

Mama and Stepdaddy's room is afore our room down the hall, and even though they share it, there's no blanket hangin' across the middle or nothin'. Anyways, there's a big bed they share in the middle of the room.

We kids ain't loud in their room by ourselves without permission, but I know Felicity don't pay no attention to me so she won't find out what I'm doin'.

They don't got a burro, only a slidin' door that opens into a closet with drawers for their clothes and whatnot and some shelves. And Mama's hat shelf has only her every day hat sittin' there. I don't know what to think 'bout this, not at all.

Mama don't wear her special hat 'cept for Sundays and Holy Days. It's kept right there on the shelf. She brushes it every week with a tiny bristly brush that she dips in cold tea. It's a fine hat. Mama married Stepdaddy in that hat, so's it's kept up and taken care of real well. It's made of thick dark green felt and has a back feather with green feathery tips tucked inside the black satin ribbon that goes all round it. I never knowed a regular day when Mama wore that there hat.

I sit down and try to figger out where Mama could go dressed up so special. I put my elbow on my knee and push up my chin with my hand to make me think harder. Everybody knows that makes the blood rush up your cheeks into your forehead, and then it sucks in your brains. I know it's true 'coz I done tested it and get nearly a hundred in every 'rithmatic test.

I look at the bottom of their closet and even her good shoes are gone. Stepdaddy's at work, so she ain't with him. It ain't Sunday, and there ain't no holiday until New Year. I saw Father John go off in his car when me and Sister were watchin' the birds. So she ain't with him. I think and think so hard, I get a headache so's I close the closet door real soft and all and go into the kitchen for a glass of juice. We each of us get a one glass of real orange juice everyday, and I forgot mine at breakfast.

Felicity's watchin' television. She could get into big trouble doin' that. Stepdaddy took the TV as part of his backpay when he left off teachin'. It didn't work real good, so Stepdaddy took it apart, and when he put it back together, it worked real fine, only a little snowy and one or two wavy black lines once on a while.

As I sit at the table to drink my juice, I wonder should I get Felicity in trouble or not. I gotta be smart and try'n remember if she has anythin' on me or not. Mama's rule is, if you have free time, read a book. We can watch one hour of television a night and Saturday mornin' cartoons.

Television still amazes Mama. She knits and looks up once on a while and says things like "Well, will you look at that!" Stepdaddy says watchin' TV through Mama's eyes makes it more excitin'. I never could figger that out. How can you look through someone else's eyes? I guess it's one of those things you learn in college, 'coz it sure don't make no sense. Anyway, I turn my chair just so's I can see a bit of the screen and still be a good boy.

At Christmas, Miss Alice invites all the kids she knows to come and watch Rudolph the Red-Nosed Reindeer in color on her color TV. The colors are real pretty and even brighter than in-life colors. I reckon she fergets there's so many kids and though she's nice and serves us orange Kool-Aid in paper cups as we sit all over her livin' room, she looks awful nervous till we leave.

Facin' our street, I can tell when Mama's comin' and decide I just won't tell Felicity when she's comin', and she'll get into trouble by herself, and it'll be outta my hands. I think it through and figger it's a real good plan. I miss seein' Jimmy; the neighbor kids play baby games and their mamas won't let them out anyhow when it's this cold out. I'm gettin' awful tired waitin' on Mama. There's just nothin' in this here big wide world for me to do.

"Bib, come see this!"

I go over to the TV and watch a newsman. Too late, I know now I'm in trouble too. I'm mad now at Felicity. But I don't say nothin' and sit next to her on the sofa to watch.

This here newsman is talkin' to another man you can see is pretty important 'coz he's wearin' a fancy suit and all under his coat. The important man looks happy and warm so's you know he's got a car with heat nearby.

"Who's that?"

"Shush. That's our mayor, and he's talking about us."

"And I have full confidence in the decision of my planning board regarding the development of this property," the mayor said. "It is something my constituents want. We have circulated an order for open bids these last three months and are currently reviewing them. We will fully realize the needs of the community when the decision is made."

"What's that mean?"

"Just hush, will you?"

"Mayor Whitehall, what made you choose this particular property east of the town's center?" the newsman asked.

"The land in question has current conveniences regarding sewerage and water, which, of course, will save costs of development. There is an easy access to the town center. The property will convert easily into a shopping center, and development would increase town revenue and open up many job opportunities for the good people of Crystal Springs."

The mayor man flashes a big white smile that I know isn't real. Seems to me like he's lookin' right at us as we sit on the sofa. And though he's smilin' at me, I don't think I trust him none. Now he's wavin', but the newsman stops him.

"One more question, Mayor Whitehall."

"Yes?" Mayor man isn't too happy. He's startin' to shiver.

"Isn't it true, sir, that the land is currently occupied, and there are groups in Minneapolis violently opposed to uprooting the current residents living in the trailer park? Isn't it true, sir, that there is town-owned land west of town that would serve the town's purpose just as well?"

Mayor man is all red now from the cold, and his words come out like they're froze.

"It is my understanding that the majority of the lots are rentals, and the property is owned by a citizen who is quite willing to sell."

"Mayor Whitehall—"

But then, more men in fancy suits and overcoats surround the mayor man, and he waves good-bye to me, this time for good.

The newsman says a few more words, his name and all, and then a commercial for Nestlé Cocoa comes on. Usually I like to watch the dog with the big floppy ears, but somehow, I don't feel like it none.

Felicity goes over to turn off the television. She moves a little closer to me on the sofa, so I know she's upset and all. Seems to me that what the mayor man said is more important than my understandin' of it.

"What did the mayor man mean, Felicity?"

"I don't know, Bib. It doesn't sound good, though."

"We'll ask Mama when she gets home." Mama understands lots of things I don't.

"Don't you dare. Then Mother will know we were watching television and we'll get it. You do a fool thing like that, and I'll lock you outdoors until you're so cold your nose freezes shut, and you'll have to breathe through your mouth and then your lungs will freeze and then you'll die."

I've heard of this afore, so I know it's true, and I shut up.

It's awful to be eight and stuck between understandin' and punishment.

CHAPTER FIVE

We go into the kitchen to start lunch, and Felicity puts a small pot of water to boil for Mama's tea. I ain't loud near the stove, but I put the teabag real careful in her favorite blue china cup. It's a real teacup straight from China, says so on the bottom. When I was little, I thought Mama had up and gone to China without me to get that cup. But no, she bought it at the church White Elephant Sale for ten cents.

Three weeks ago, I done broke the blue saucer that went to that cup. That was the first and last time I was loud to stay home alone. Miss Alice had dropped Dill off to play with me, and when I loosened the shoelaces on my red Keds for him to catch, we ran right round the livin' room and then right into the kitchen, half round the table since it's pushed gainst the wall and next thing I know that saucer was right on the floor in three pieces. I was scared 'coz nothin' like that had ever happened to me afore. Dill just stopped still, looked at the floor, then at me, and jumped on the sofa to wash hisself. I was kinda mad at him for leavin' me there alone, but Dill knew I done it 'coz he weren't tall enough to bump into that counter.

Quick, I got the Elmer's Glue and put that saucer together best I could. There was white globs of glue, and when I went to wash it off, the whole thing fell apart again. After a while, it stuck and I put it back on the counter, put the teacup on top, and then took Dill to my room to lie on my bed.

It was an awful long time afore anybody got home. Dill slept fine, and I just rubbed his fluffy belly and tried to think of somethin 'sides that cup. I heard the door open, voices full of gladness 'coz they was home outta the cold, and everythin' was fine, and that saucer wasn't busted.

Mama started gettin' supper ready. Stepdaddy told her a funny story to make her laugh. I heard runnin' water then that awful silence I was waitin' for.

Too soon, there's a knock on my door, and Stepdaddy comes in. I sat up in bed and tried real hard to look like a little boy who would never break a china saucer.

"Bib, what were you doing while Mama and I were out?"

"Played with Dill." I scooped him up and hugged him to me on my lap. He was real dead weight, what with his head, arms, legs, and tail floppin' everywhere and all. He didn't want to be part of this, no way at all. I couldn't blame him none, but friends should stick together. Stepdaddy sat down on my bed and petted Dill.

"What else?"

"Nothin' much."

"Did you play ball in the house?"

"No."

"Run around?"

"No."

"Bib, you're a good boy. You know we love you. Now I'm going to give you one more chance to tell the truth. Did you break that saucer?"

"Yes, Stepdaddy." So I told him what happened.

"Well, you will go into the kitchen, tell your Mama and apologize."

"Yessir." I got up to go.

"Wait." Stepdaddy stands up and gets somethin' from his pocket of his worn denim work pants. Then he sits me close to him and holds out a roof nail. It's a little longer than my little finger and has a slanty side. He put the nail in my hand and closed my fingers round it.

"Next time you think about lying, son, you take this from your pocket and look at it. Lying is as much of a sin as stealing or anything else and all these sins, whether big or small are the nails that put our Savior on the cross."

I feel the weight of it in my hand.

"I'm sorry, Stepdaddy."

"I know you are, Bib. And that makes me proud." He hugs me and tells me to go see Mama.

I kept that nail in my pocket for an awful long time; it got real comfortable livin' with my bits of string, marbles, die, and washers.

Wednesday recesses, me and Johnny Whitt have swap meets on the stairs by the back dooryard of the school. Johnny and me learn math together, though mostly I learn and he copies from my papers. I can't say nothin' 'coz we're friends. You don't snitch on friends. That's a good way to get awful hurt. Anyway, one day I emptied my pocket, and Johnny spied that nail right away. I knew from the start he wanted it 'coz he laughed at me for carryin' round an old nail. Washers, well, you can do somethin' with them.

Then I told him Stepdaddy's story and all, and he was real impressed. Now he wanted that nail awful bad. So much that he done traded me a real glass shooter for it, the kind that have that wavy blue color goin' through it. Him and me crossed ourselves and shook hands on the deal.

Now, when I think of lyin', I take out the shooter and look at it real hard. I reckon it works just as well as the nail did.

So now I'm lookin' at Mama's cup, and I know if she comes home with her "Mama Instinct," she's gonna ask me what I've been doin'. And I'm gonna have to tell her, freezin' lung death or not.

The door opens, and Mama comes in bringin' in fresh cold air, and her cheeks are red, and she's full of smiles. Her carrybags are full of small and big packages, and we help her put them on the table.

While she's takin' off her coat, she's talkin' and happy, and Felicity asks why she didn't tell us she was goin' shoppin' 'coz we coulda met her at the bus stop and helped her carry things home.

"It was only a bit of a walk and did me good."

"What is all this?"

"Wait until I put my hat away."

Turns out the carrybags are full of groceries. There's a pack of sugar and a small gunnysack of flour that Mr. Samson on Shirley Street sells for people who can't afford a big bag of Robin Hood Flour but would like to bake a little somethin' anyway. There's a big white paper package of cube steak and an onion to cook with it to make it taste like real meat. There's even two bottles of pop for me and Felicity—cream soda, which I like best.

I'm wonderin' if maybe Mama's goin' only a little bit outta her mind. Maybe it's the cold.

"My, that tea smells good." She sits at the table and takes a sip. To get some of the cold outta her cheeks, she holds the side of the cup to her face. "You children hurry and eat your lunch, sandwiches, mind, nothing messy. Then I'm going to make a cake."

"A cake? Christmas is over, and we're gonna have a cake?"

"Yes, Bib. A good supper and apple cake for dessert. We've got some celebrating to do tonight."

"What celebrating?" Felicity is gettin' out the bread and peanut butter while I find a knife and the jelly.

"Never you mind. You'll have to wait until your father gets home. And no guessing."

I think that's a silly thing to say, but I don't say nothin'. I can't think of nothin' that could give Mama the idea to make a cake. Felicity is thinkin' real hard as she puts dishes in the sink and looks at Mama once on a while.

CHAPTER SIX

That there supper was one of the best we ever had, even including Christmas. Mama made light biscuits, and we even had a small jar of honey so's we could spread it on top. We had stewed tomatoes on the side with little dried green things in them that taste better than they look. The whole place was full of good smells of the coffee perkin' on the stove, apple cake, cinnamon, and the Christmas tree.

Stepdaddy and Mama were smilin' and laughin' a lot, so much that they didn't correct my table manners. I tried it to see. I reached way across the table for the honey, and nobody said nothin' to me. That's how I knowed Stepdaddy knew the secret, and to my way of thinkin', it ain't fair he got told the surprise afore me.

We each had a big slice of that cake, oozin' with sugar cinnamon syrup and apple slices. Me and Felicity even had our own cups of coffee, her's blacker than mine, but mine more sugary.

Finally Mama says, "Your Daddy and I have something to tell you." Her eyes are dark and bright shinin'. She holds Stepdaddy's hand and says, "We're going to have a new baby."

After we helped Felicity swallow the coffee she done choked on, then we could talk some.

"When?" I ask.

"Well, Bib, Dr. Maitland thinks around the middle of July."

"Mother! Where are we going to keep a baby? This trailer is tiny enough with the four of us living here. Bib and I are already sharing a room which is embarrassing enough at my age, after all I'm fifteen, and I do need my privacy—"

"Felicity Mary, you just hush right now. There's time enough to plan for that, and we won't go borrowing worry before then." With Mama usin' her warnin' eyes and middle names and all, I'd shut up if I was Felicity. She knows it too, so she does.

"I'm sorry, Mother."

Stepdaddy is lookin' at us and lookin' worried. All the gladness seems to have left.

"We thought you'd be pleased," he said.

"I am." I took a big bite of cake. "I'm gonna be glad to have a little brother. And I don't see why we have to wait all the way to July. We should get him from Dr. Maitland now. July's an awful long ways away, and 'sides it's so hot, if we get him now, he'd grow up some by then, and we could go swimmin' in Lark's Pond."

"Oh, Bib." Mama's laughin' again.

"And what if it's a little sister?" asks Stepdaddy.

I looks over at Felicity and see that she's all upset again but tryin' not to show it. And I think on the giggly way she acts with her friends and her complainin' and fussin' on clothes and such. I shake my head and tell 'em, "I don't reckon God would do that to me again."

"Congratulations, Mother." Felicity pinches my leg under the table, and I reckon I'm in for trouble later.

"Thank you, Felicity. Now, perhaps you'll help me clean up after supper." She gets up, but afore she touches even a plate, Felicity says, "No, Mother. I'm sorry about what I said. I'm really very happy about the baby. You go relax and I'll do the dishes." Felicity starts clearin' the table and clatterin' dishes in the sink. I think on acting big like that and offerin' to help, but that idea don't seem to last too long in my head. 'Sides, she did pinch me.

On the sofa, Stepdaddy tucks a blanket round Mama and sits close to her. He done put more wood in the stove and it's nice and warm.

Mama says, "Let's look in the Pride Box. Bib, go into the bedroom and mind you be careful. You know where it is."

I always like lookin' at the Pride Box. Mama started it some time ago when Felicity was little. It's a square tin box, long ago painted red and black, but now looks more like solder. One time Felicity was showin' off what she learned in school and came home and told Mama pride was a sin, so we should throw that box away. I was real little, but I still remember I was scared 'coz I thought Mama would agree with Felicity and throw it out. But she just said, "I'm well aware pride is a sin, Felicity. But what we have in here is a different kind of pride. Sinful pride can't be kept in a box. It's right there in the open for anyone to see. The things we have in this box represent pride in our family, our accomplishments and pride in each other."

So the box stayed.

When Felicity came from the kitchen, we all sat round to look inside the box. On top was a white rose, dried but protected in wax paper. Mama carried that rose when she married Stepdaddy. She opened it and said, "Look. You can still smell it." We passed it round and each took a smell of waxy rose. Some of the stuff in the Pride Box is kinda borin' to me, like Grandma's wooden rosary and some tickets and mushy stuff that Mama collected while Stepdaddy dated her. We reread Stepdaddy's letter of resination from his old teachin' job. Mama folded it real careful and put it aside.

We laughed, even Felicity, when we came on her Confirmation picture. Dressed all in white like a little bride, she's squintin' at the camera, and we can barely make out her face. We looked at her old report cards, and then the pictures I drewed during our long car trip from Tennessee to Minnesota, one for each state. Mama likes to admire them, and I know they're good. We had a long drive ahead of us, and Felicity and me, we were bored afore we left the state line of Tennessee. Round bout Kentucky, Stepdaddy told us if we asked if we were there yet one more time, he'd turn round. That's when Mama gave me paper and crayons to draw pictures.

We had to drive through three big states afore we reached Minnesota. Stepdaddy's car was none too new, but it was squishy comfortable in back. The stuffin' came out and made a fine pillow for sleepin'. We camped along the way. Stepdaddy had to stop a lotta times to put water in the radiator. We had all kindsa containers filled with water in that car. I was sure sorry when Stepdaddy sold that car for scrap metal after we got to Minnesota.

Anyway, I drewed our family drivin' away from the ugly brick Tennessee building once and all. For Kentucky, I drew a horse. I was kinda stumped on Illinois until Mama reminded me Abraham Lincoln was from there, so I drewed him. Iowa was easy, corn all over the place.

Mama held the map open that we were followin', and Minnesota looked awful big 'paired to Tennessee. Above Minnesota was a whole big area in light-green color.

"What's that?" I asked, pointin' to it.

"That's Canada."

"Is that a big state?"

"No, Bib, it's a whole different country from here,"— she pointed—"to here."

I sat back in the seat and thought on this. I reckon you can't go no further north and still be American than where we was goin'. And above our new home sits a big huge country that weren't even part of us. And I thought it was a mighty fine thing to move to this state of Minnesota 'coz if we got bored and such we could always drive up some and visit foreign folks for a while.

Mama finds what she's lookin' for in the Pride Box, a long lacy baptizin' dress that me and Felicity both wored when we was babies. It's gotten a little yellowy, but Mama reckons she can make it white again. She's fingerin' the lace real gentle, and she says, "For our baby." She and Stepdaddy kiss each other under a hangin' bow of the tree, and I figger this is a Christmas I'll never ferget, even if I live to be forty.

That was such an excitin' night that I hoped when Mama tucked me in, she'd ferget bout my night diction lesson. But no, she sits on my bed and starts.

"All right, Bib, here we go. You've been doing so well, and we're so proud of you. Now repeat after me. Riding."

"Ridin'."

"Riding."

"Ridin'. I mean, riding."

"Wonderful! Now repeat ing, ing, ing."

"Mama."

"Go ahead, dear."

"Ing, ing, ing."

"Now use a word that ends in *ing*."

"Riding."

"Think of another word."

I pause, then think, and say, "Sledding."

"Good. Now repeat this sentence. I saw them at the store."

"Saw 'em at the store."

"I saw them at the store."

"I saw 'em at the store." I just can't get that durn *th* sound out.

"Put your tongue between your teeth. That's how we make the *th* sound."

I try it and finally say, "Them." This feels like it's goin' on forever. Then I hear again Mama's lecture 'bout *ain't*.

Finally, she kisses me good night. I lay in bed thinkin' on the new baby comin', and it's a real happy feelin'. Durin' prayers, I said a special thanks 'coz there's gonna be a baby brother to play with.

Then I remember my composition I have to write for Sister Mary Margaret. I reckon I'd better start tomorrow 'coz it's gonna be awful hard and take a lotta time to write one hundred words. I don't know if I've ever seen one hundred words at one time on one page. It's just not fair. Still, it's better than Mama knowin' 'bout my slangshot.

In the dark, I hear the wind outdoors rushin' long the road. My bedtime is 8:00, which ain't bad, isn't bad, in winter, but in summer, it's still light out, and I can hear other kids playin' outdoors. Even littler kids than me. They know which window's mine, and sometimes, they whisper stuff to tease me. I can't shut the window 'coz it gets sufferable hot in that trailer in the summer. I just lie there and think on how I'm goin' to get 'em tomorrow, things I mostly ferget when I wake up. Winter or summer, I wait to sleep anyway till I hear the train movin' up to Coon Rapids. I like the sound of the wheels on the track as it runs by and the long whistle that says good night to me. I like think it's my very own train. I saw that there train in person once. We went to the Coon Rapids' drive-in movie with a friend of Stepdaddy's. They have to stop the movie when the train comes through. Some folks complain 'bout that, but I like the train better than the movie.

Tonight, the whistle is long and very clear in the thin cold air. I reckon it's a special message just for me, to congradulate me on bein' a big brother.

CHAPTER SEVEN

This mornin', I'm thinking on "The Beauty of God's Creation" and wonderin' how I'm gonna get one hundred words outta just that. Sister near always tells us to write what we'd like, but we really know that means write what she wants to hear. Teachers are like that, if you write what you like you're more'n likely to get a bad mark.

Mostly, I like school. It's surely a lot easier to get long with all the other kids than two years ago September. First day Mama signed me up, they put me in Sister Mary Alloysha's kindergarten class.

I didn't like bein' with the babies and neither did Mama and Stepdaddy. I was six and ready to learn real stuff. Mama wanted to go right down and talk to them, but Stepdaddy told her to "wait and see" and "let Bib prove himself," which took longer than I 'spected it to.

One day, I was readin' a book and stayin' away from the other kids in the playground. Most of the girls were playin' at being mamas and the boys had a box of rusty Matchbox cars. Some of 'em only had three wheels, so they pretended those cars were in accidents. I kinda woulda liked to play with those boys, but at that time, they were still laughin' at me, so I couldn't.

Sister Mary Alloysha came to me and sat down for a spell.

"Robert, don't you want to go over and play with the other children?"

"No, ma'am. I mean, no, thank you, ma'am. I'd rather read."

"But, Robert, I will be readin' to the class after playtime. You can see the pictures then."

"Yes, ma'am, I mean I surely enjoy hearin' you read and all, but sometimes, I like to read a bit myself. 'Sides, playtime's early today, and I didn't know if you'd be readin' next or if we was gonna do somethin' else."

Sister stared on me a long time, a uncomfortable stare that made me look down at my hands hopin' I remembered to wash 'em good that mornin'.

"Robert, will you read to me the first sentence of that book?"

"Yes, ma'am." I flipped back the pages and started on readin'.

Finally, she says, "That's enough, Robert." Then she looked at the big clock on the wall and asked me the time. I told her it was 12:45.

"Robert, can you add three and four?"

"Course I can. That'd be seven, Sister."

Sister Mary Alloysha stood up and lookin' down at me she smiled and told me I was a very smart boy. Then she turned to the class and told the other kids she'd be right back; she had to see the Mother Superior. She told 'em to be good and play nice and all, and with her lookin' at 'em like that, you knew they would. She took my hand, and we went out into the cool hallway.

I got real nervous. I went over and over in my head what I talked about with Sister and didn't know what I did, so I ask, "Sister, did I do somethin' wrong?"

"No, Robert." She hugged me there in the hallway. "Let's go see Mother Superior."

Mother and Sister talked a long time while I sat outside the closed door on the long hard wood bench. The back of it was slatted wood, and as time went on, I felt like those slats was wearin' in my back. My feet started to buzz, the way feet do when they fall asleep. Finally, they called me in.

The tall chair I sat in cross from Mother's desk made me feel real little and bad.

"Good morning, Robert."

Over her head was a big crucifix with bright red paint in all the bloody spots. It scared me some, so I had trouble lookin' at Mother's face.

"Mornin', Mother Mary Robert."

"Well, Robert, Sister Mary Alloysha tells me you're a very smart young man for your age. How old are you now?" She reached for some papers on her desk.

"Six, goin' on seven in January, Mother."

"Where did you learn to read and tell time? Your record shows you didn't attend a school before this year."

Mother didn't sound near as mean as the other kids told me. I stopped bein' so scared and hitched myself up higher by sittin' on my foot, so we could talk more eye to eye. I done told her 'bout how I weren't loud to go to kindergarten in Tennessee. It was too far for me to walk, and Mama didn't want me to anyway. Mama didn't drive, and there weren't no buses. So when Mama took me with her to work she'd give me knobbly pencils and bits of paper. I had lots of fun practicing my alphabet and my numbers on those papers. And how Mama helped me read at night afore bed. Then Mama told me it would surely be a help if I could tell her the time now and again, so I learned to read time on the clock, which is awful hard. I told Mother how clocks have three hands, and you gotta keep track of each one. I just kept on tryin' till I learned it.

After a while, Mother told me good afternoon, and I said I surely enjoyed talkin' to her, 'specially since I got outta playtime.

Sister Mary Alloysha led me to another room. "Sit still now, Robert, while I go and get Sister Mary Luke. I must go back to class."

"Yes, ma'am." All the nuns here have the same first name. Mary. I wonder on this a lot, but I don't ask no questions 'coz that might be rude. It might really bother 'em. I wouldn't like to be in a house full of Roberts. The room is small and hot, with little kid tables, and I laid my head down. It was wearyin' talkin' for such a long time. I sang "The Tennessee Waltz" under my breath while my head was down.

The door opened.

"I am Sister Mary Luke." Somethin' in her voice made me sit up real straight.

"I teach second grade here at St. Francis."

"Yes, ma'am."

"You were in the wrong class."

"Yes, ma'am, and I'm surely sorry 'bout that."

"An apology is not yours to make, young man. Now, here is a test you are to take, and I will give you twenty minutes, no more and no less, to complete it. This test will inform me if you should be placed in the first or the second grade. Begin."

That test was kinda fun. As I worked it, I felt like I was finally in school. I was awful sick of playin' all day long and lookin' at baby books. I made circles and squares, read some stories, and answered questions 'bout 'em, added numbers and such.

"Time is up." Sister put her hand out, and I gave her my paper. She looked at it, read it through, and made some marks with a red pencil.

"Beginning tomorrow, Robert Harper, you will join my second-grade class. Please be punctual. You will have a lot of work to make up."

"Yes, ma'am."

"You will now rejoin your class for the remainder of the day."

"Yes, ma'am. Thank you, ma'am."

When I got back to the class, I was just in time for readin'. The other kids stared at me, probably 'coz they were wonderin' if I got a whippin' with the ruler on my hands. Sister Mary Alloysha welcomed me back, and I went to my seat. On purpose, I put my hands palm up on the table so's they could see I weren't no bad boy bein' punished. I didn't really listen to the story 'bout the farmer's cow. I was thinkin' on how it would be different tomorrow. I'd get readin' books and learn 'rithmatic and have those little blue books to write in. Probably my own pencil, too.

I guessed I done proved myself that day, just like Stepdaddy said.

CHAPTER EIGHT

There comes a terrible cold snap, and the wind is whompin' the trailer as bad as it's whippin' the branches outdoors. Our bedroom is like one frozen ice cube. Even the insides of the windows has frost on 'em and little slivers of ice.

I decide to write my composition on the kitchen table next to the stove. Felicity is helpin' Mama clean the livin' room, brushin' up needles from the floor that fell offa my tree. The tress is gone. I don't even ask when they took it down 'coz that would give Felicity a chance to sneer at me. Anyway, the smell is still round me.

At the table, I line up my pencils and paper, wastin' time just thinkin' on how I can come up with one hundred words. I'm wonderin' if I can count all the little words like *the* and *and*. That would take up an awful lot of those hundred words. Then I remember the title and counted them. Five whole words right there. I feel much better 'coz that means I only have to write ninety-five words, so I just start writin' without countin', 'coz countin' will drive you crazy.

I'm writin' on Tennessee stead a Minnesota, 'coz I do miss it even if I say I don't. Anyway, right now, all I can think of is snow 'bout Minnesota. Snow is pretty, but not very many critters come out in these parts when there's a lotta snow. 'Cept birds and squirrels, and though I like 'em and all, it's not much to write on. And I don't wanna write none on Florence, where we lived when I was little, 'coz that was a town without much to it. So I write on Red Brick, the old old town we left behind in Tennessee. It's where Mama's brother lived and Felicity and me lived with him awhile while Mama worked. We lived close enough to the Watauga River to go fishin' or swimmin' whenever we wanted, when Mama said we could and we had a grownup with us.

Cypress trees grew long the river and at a time Mama calls twilight, which comes every day, their shaggy gray-green beards of Spanish Moss made 'em look like giants waitin' on eatin' us. So we never stayed long after the sun started to go down. I write about this, and the black bears we saw scratchin' their backs on the trees, the possums and coons crawlin' through the trees at night, and the salamanders we'd catch for pets. Once I even saw a bobcat sunnin' hisself on a rock. Mama was with me that day; otherwise, I might have tried to pet him. Mama says even though wild animals are furry and cute, they can be dangerous. When I looked at that bobcat's face, I didn't know whether I believed this or not. But Mama's never lied to me afore so I reckon it's true.

I remember thinkin' in the winter how much fun the kids up north must have in winter, 'coz we hardly got no snow in Tennessee. But I never reckoned there could be so much snow at one time like in this here Minnesota. And so much cold neither. Our first winter here, why, I thought everybody would freeze right to death.

Anyway, in Red Brick, we all lived with Uncle Sey and Aunty Mercy. The Blue Ridge Mountains seemed to be everywhere. I liked those mountains an awful lot. They were big and pretty blue. They were there a long, long time, I ferget how long. It's a comfortably feelin' knowin' those mountains have been right there in that place, and they won't move none.

Uncle Sey had a tobacco farm west of the river. Mama would catch the bus from Red Brick to Jonesborough to work durin' the week at a hotel and come back on weekends. Plantin' and harvestin' times, she'd stay with us in the cabin and help out Uncle Sey and Aunty Mercy. The hotel people would let her off durin' those times.

Uncle Sey's real name is Uncle Seymour and Aunty Mercy's real name is Aunty Mae. Neither one uses their real names; it was all settled afore Felicity was borned. Aunty Mercy was called that 'coz she said "mercy" so much. But Uncle Sey just hates the name Seymour.

'Sides he says when folks call out "Hey, Sey," they can't help but laugh, which makes 'em like him more.

Uncle Sey is bigger than any man I ever done see. Even bigger'n his brother Andrew. Uncle Sey has big hands what can break a branch from a tree for kindlin', but they're gentle hands too what likes to feel new kitten fur. Aunty Mercy always says Uncle Sey had a soft spot for every critter on earth. Their farm is full of animals that Uncle Sey rescued from the woods or the river. He'd nurse 'em back to health until they could live on their own. Course, meanwhiles, they'd get awful attached to Uncle Sey and wouldn't wanna go. And Uncle Sey would keep sayin' those critters aren't ready to go none. Soon after that, they'd become pets and we could play with most of 'em. He rescued a big blue heron once that had a hurt wing. That heron followed Uncle Sey round the barnyard when he was collectin' manure for fertilizin' the fields. That heron acted like a tall, gawky kid, just like Felicity. It would nuzzle Uncle Sey's pocket with his big beak, lookin' for the cracked corn he knew was always there. In the mornin', Uncle Sey and Aunty Mercy would wake up to the grackle voice of the heron callin' to Uncle Sey right under his window. What with the roosters and other animals makin' so much noise, nobody even tried to go back to sleep after they woke up.

Aunty Mercy did try to put her foot down when the pig was brought home. Uncle Sey told her the pig would be a vestment, prices of pork bein' so high and all. He reminded Aunty Mercy how much she did love a barbeque now and then. She just looked at him and sighed. She told him to take the pig outta the house and put him in a pen, and she didn't want to hear one more word 'bout it till butcherin' time.

Uncle Sey and me saved lots of extra scraps to feed the pig. He was awful cute, pink, and squiggly and a lot of fun to play with. Even the dogs played with him, but not the cats. We even found him curled up and asleep next to Myra, the donkey. That pig sure grew fast, though. Once on a while, Aunty Mercy would ask when the pig would be ready for butcherin', but it never seemed the right time. When Uncle Sey named the pig Hugs, we all knew it was over, and Hugs became another member of the family.

Farmin' was hard work for everybody. Uncle Sey only had an acre, but it kept the family goin'. Uncle Andy lived down the road a bit and helped. Uncle Andy weren't married or nothin', so I reckon he had plenty of time. They spent most of their time from September to January splittin' wood and haulin' big old branches outta the woods. Uncle Sey needed that wood to heat the cabin and to cure the tobacco in late summer. Uncle Sey showed me how to use the cross-cut saw, but he always lifted me offa my feet when it was his turn to draw the saw toward him.

In January, Felicity and me watched the men burn the plant beds to get 'em ready for the new seeds. Aunty Mercy would be hangin' outta the window most of the time, tellin' us to be careful. If we were even a little bit near the flames, her blue checked duster would wave like a crazy flag, and someone would come to yell at us to move on.

After the burnin' was the fun time. We got to stomp the seeds real good into the ground. Uncle Sey would put on the radio, and we'd dance near all the day long up and down the plant beds and have a real good time. Then we'd help stretch the white cloth over to protect the little seeds from the wind and such, so that they'd grow into big strong plants.

Mama would come home weekends, tired from her week of cleanin' at the Spencer Hotel. Once on a time, she'd have extra tips from the folks who stayed there, and maybe we'd take in a movie at the movie house in Elkwood. Elkwood is a fancy town on the Watauga River, where all the rich folks have their summer houses. We'd never stay round much after the movie, 'coz those people didn't like strangers comin' in their town.

In May, Mama would be home for a whole week. Uncle Sey had lots of friends, and they'd help us durin' plantin' time. We'd start transplantin' the tiny little plants into the field. You have to be real gentle to those plants; their little leaves can be bruised if you don't handle 'em right. We would follow one another, singin' and tellin' stories and laughin'. Uncle Sey would dig a hole, I got to put the water into the hole, and Mama would place the plant. Over in the next furrow, Aunty Mercy, Felicity and Uncle Andy would be doin' the same thing. And all Uncle Sey's friends would help him for no pay. He'd give 'em a big party at the end of Saturday plantin' when we'd be done. By Saturday, we'd set near 8,000 tobacco plants.

I was four and wanted to be just like Uncle Sey. Big and strong and ownin' my own tobacco farm. But then, the summer would start and all the hard dirty work under the hot sun made everybody tired and kinda grumpy at night. We'd plow and hoe that field enough to know each plant by name.

Sometimes, Uncle Sey would take me for a walk to the little store where he bought his beer, and he'd get me a Mountain Dew. We'd both open our cans for the walk back 'coz our throats would be dry and dirty. Long 'bout the bend of the road, he'd put the rest of his cans in an old log that he hollered out afore we went home. Aunty Mercy would come over to us, usually dryin' her hands on an apron. She could smell the beer on Uncle Sey's breath, but she never did catch him with one in his hand. She'd sniff him up and down with an awful mad look, and then she'd laugh and say, "Oh, you!" and go back into the kitchen.

Then there'd come a time when the big black cauldron would come out by the dooryard, and Aunty Mercy would begin boilin' water and never seem to stop. This was round bout June, and the tobacco would be waist high to a man, and we'd start the real hard work. The kinda work that makes you want to be a fisherman and leave the land alone. We'd hafta top the plants and sucker 'em. Aunty Mercy had a special shelf in her outhouse where she'd put a clean change of clothes for us after a day in the fields. We'd hafta change our clothes, wash up in an old dishpan full of rain water, and put our dirty clothes into the boilin' water.

Aunty Mercy couldn't abide tobacco gum. It weren't loud in her house. She fought that gum like she was in a war.

What with the cauldron boilin', and the fires goin' at both ends of the curin' barns, it was terrible hot there. We would all be glad when harvestin' was over, and the crop was taken to market in Vernon to sell. The buyers always made a good show over Uncle Sey's tobacco; he grew the best in all County Carteret.

Long time ago, when Mama's name was Claire and not Mama, she went with her daddy and mama to market to sell tobacco. That was when they'd sell at Mullwood Market, almost the biggest in the whole state. Everyone would go there and stay over in camps. They'd play cards, or sing and dance and have an awful good time. That was when Uncle Simon was still alive, Uncle Seymour's twin brother. Uncle Simon was courtin' a girl named Rita who lived in Mullwood. They all went out one night, Andy, Sey, and Simon. Their daddy, Grandaddy Bob, told them to be sure to be back by the ten o'clock curfew. Everybody had to be home at ten o'clock. I reckon adults had a bedtime back then.

Uncle Simon never made it back. They found him next mornin' dead with a bullet in his head. All of them cried when they brought Uncle Simon home to be buried. Rita wanted to come back with them, but her family wouldn't let her. They were some scared; word'd get round that Rita was courtin' a lawless boy. Grandaddy Bob told 'em the boy weren't lawless, only the men what made the laws were. Anyway, Rita's family was real sorry about Uncle Simon, they gave a basket of flowers for the funeral that was so fancy, Uncle Seymour can describe it to this day.

Writin' about the beauty of God's Creation in Tennessee makes me wonder why I feel so sad of a sudden.

I count the words in my composition, and I have 'zactly one hundred and twenty. When I cross those off that are on Sister Mary Margaret's list I still have over a hundred.

Then I copy it over in good handwritin' and show it to Mama. She likes it real well, but looks kinda sad too, just like me. Mama says my writing is beautiful, and my grammar is gettin' better all the time. She says soon I'll be talkin' as well as Stepdaddy and Felicity. Felicity studies awful hard to talk proper. She says that talkin' good will make her way in the world.

That night, after the train said good night, I was still too worked up to sleep. I sing soft to myself, "Ing, ing, ing."

CHAPTER NINE

Yesterday was January 30, my birthday. I am nine years old. We usually have a real small birthday party for me, 'coz it's the day afore New Year's Eve and that's the big party. When I was little, I thought everyone was celebratin' my birthday just one day late. But no, they was celebratin' the New Year. Anyway, I sorta pretend it's for me too.

Mama had strung up blue streamers, and there was balloons blowed up and tied to the kitchen chairs. In the middle of the table was a plate of brownies, oozing with chocolate. And round that, birthday presents for me.

My favorite present was from Miss Alice. It was a stuffed cat that looked 'zactly like Dill. I know I'm kinda big for a stuffed animal. But it's almost like havin' a cat of my own. Mama and Stepdaddy gave me a new Hardy Book to read, a new shirt and some pants. They always give clothes for birthdays. Then Felicity hands me a package, all wrapped up and all. I open it and it's a Slinky toy.

Now that surprised me.

Felicity and me don't hardly ever get long. I always figgered she didn't like me, what with all the names she calls me and such. And we never play 'coz she's so much older'n me. Once, when I really bugged her to play she asked did I wanna play war. I said course I do. She had me lay by the willer tree and be a dead soldier. I waited there so long, I fell asleep. I can tell you I was awful mad when I woke up.

But once, in Red Brick, she stood up for me in a big way. Mama had let us walk uptown, and we had a whole nickel to share to buy somethin'. A bunch of boys began followin' us. Felicity was nervous and told me to walk faster. I tried, but I had little legs back then. Then I guess one boy called me a bad name 'coz Felicity just stopped and spun round.

"What did you say?"

"I was talkin' to your brother, you stupid dog."

I said, "Let's just go, Felicity."

"No, Bib. Stay out of this." Felicity starts to walk over to 'em. There's 'bout five boys there and they are all taller than my sister and seem awful big to me. But she ain't scared none, her fists are curled up and she's walkin' steady-like. I'm scared. Felicity looks mean but so small. She's only eleven and those boys look older. All of the boys had their summer buzz hair cuts which make them look and act tougher than they really are. One of 'em had the reddest hair I ever seen; I'd never ferget it. I remember they were all laughin' real hard watching my sister walk over to 'em. The closer she got to them, the less they was smilin'.

She done walked right up to that boy's face, the one who called me a bad name. All the other boys weren't so brave, now. Some of 'em ran away.

"Apologize to my brother," said Felicity looking straight at him.

He stops laughing and starts to look mad. He wrinkles up his nose at her and his hands become like fists, too, just like hers. But bigger. "No. You can't make me."

"I sure can. Apologize."

The boy gives her a little push and says, "Get out of here, dog."

Afore I knew it, Felicity done hit that boy right in the face with her fist. I just stood there with my mouth open. The boy fell down right in the dirt road and she kicked him. "Apologize!"

There was a scuffle, but the boy knew he wouldn't win, what with Felicity sittin' on his chest and slappin' him and all. She was like a spitfire.

"I'm sorry," he screamed. She gave him one more shake then got up.

"Don't you,"—she was huffin' and still mad—"don't you ever bother my brother again."

"Okay, okay. Jeeze." The boy rolled away from her and got up. He wiped down the dirt on his pants and said, "You're going to be in big trouble."

"Good." Felicity took my hand and we started walkin' uptown.

I didn't know what to say. I didn't even hear what that there boy called me. When I asked, Felicity told me it didn't matter.

"Well, why'd you fight him then?"

"Because."

"Because why?"

"Listen, Bib. If you keep quiet about this at home and stop asking questions, we'll spend the whole nickel on an ice cream cone for you."

"Honest?"

"Honest."

We had a real good time that day, Felicity and me. We walked on down to the Five and Dime and looked at all the toys. Seems to me that there place had more toys than I ever did see. Felicity told me there were bigger stores than this, but I didn't believe her. There was army men, little cars and big trucks, balls, kites in most any color you can think of, wooden planes you can fly and models. Course there was little girl stuff, too, but I didn't look on that.

"I want an army truck," I told Felicity.

"I thought you wanted an ice cream cone."

"Can't we get both?"

"No, Bib."

"Oh."

Looked like I had to make a choice. I hate that. If I pick somethin' afterwards I near always change my mind, but it's too late. So we cross the street and go into the ice cream parlor. There was two lines to get ice cream, it bein' so hot and all. We waited at the counter forever, while the man made cones for the kids in the other line. Finally, he came to us and asked us what we wanted.

"One small vanilla cone, please." Felicity knew I always liked that flavor the best. The man stared at her. He asked if she had a nickel, lookin' like he didn't believe her.

"Yes." She handed him the nickel.

We went outdoors and sat on a bench for us, and I licked that cone, and it tasted mighty fine. I thought about what Felicity done earlier. "Let's share," I said, handing her the cone. Together, we licked it all the way to the bottom, rippin' off pieces of cone and eatin''em.

When we was done, we were all sticky. I wanted to go back inside and wash up some, but Felicity didn't want to. So we headed back home.

Once we're inside, we feel a little cooler, 'coz lots of trees shade the cabin.

I was colorin' and Felicity was readin' a book when I looked out the window and saw a cloud of dirt and dust. "Somebody's comin'," I yell. Maybe Mama's come home early. We watch the driveway, and a lady gets outta one side of the car, and a boy follows her. They came up the steps, and we heard knockin' on the door. I went to the door and there stood a mad lookin' lady with that boy what Felicity beat up.

The lady looked down on me and asked if my mama was home.

"No, ma'am. Mama's at work."

"Who is watching you, then?"

"My Aunty Mercy."

"Then go get her, boy, I want to talk to her."

"Yes, ma'am." I find Aunty Mercy in the kitchen. "Aunty Mercy, a lady is here to see you."

"Lady? What lady?"

Now this here lady must be the boy's mama. I don't know how to tell her this without tellin' her about Felicity fightin'. So I just says a lady is at the front door. Aunty Mercy wipes her hands on her red checked apron and follows me.

"May I help you?" Aunty Mercy asks her. She looks confused.

"You certainly can help me. That girl over there,"— she points at Felicity—"beat up my son when he was with friends uptown. I want to know what you're going to do about it."

"I'm sorry?"

"I said your daughter, or niece, or whatever she is, hit my son deliberately."

Aunty Mercy stands taller. "That is my niece, Felicity."

"Her name doesn't matter. She beat up my son."

Aunty Mercy turned round and told Felicity to come to her. I watch her. There's no expression on Felicity's face at all.

"Yes, ma'am?" she said to the lady.

"Don't you 'yes, ma'am' me. I want to know why you beat up my son, and I want an apology. Right now."

"You can't talk to my niece that way."

"I certainly can. She's nothing more than a hoodlum."

"Felicity, did you hit this boy?"

"Yes, Aunty Mercy."

"Well, for heaven's sake, why? You know better than to hit someone."

Felicity is quiet and don't answer her.

"I didn't do nothing to neither of them," said the boy with a fake sniff like he's cryin'.

"Felicity? Please explain yourself." Aunt Mercy is usin' her stern voice. But Felicity still won't say nothin'.

Finally, Aunty Mercy says to the lady, "I am sorry, ma'am. I will deal with this. I can assure you."

"No. I want that girl to apologize to my son. You're lucky I didn't go to the police, and I'm not saying I won't go now."

"The police? For a scuffle between two children? That's rather harsh."

"It's not harsh at all. Your niece accosted my son. That is criminal behavior."

"Criminal? Felicity, why did you hit this boy? Now, you answer me right now."

"He called Bib a bad name."

"What name? What did he say?"

"I didn't say anything," the boy shouted.

"You see? My son did nothing, yet that girl hit him. More than once."

"Felicity, what did he say?"

But Felicity won't answer.

"Bib," says Aunty Mercy. She looks like she's goin' to cry, but she's startin' to look mad too. I'm wonderin' on who she's mad at and hopin' it's not me. Sounds like I started all this fuss, and I don't even know why or how. "What did the boy say to you?"

I feel miserable, 'coz I really want to help Felicity out. But I hafta say, "Aunty Mercy, I don't know. I didn't hear him."

"I can see one of them doesn't lie, at least," says the lady, "and it's obviously a lie when the boy didn't hear anything himself."

Felicity is feelin' bad for Aunty Mercy, so she looks on the lady and says, "I am sorry, ma'am."

"Well, don't apologize to me, girl, apologize to my son."

Felicity looks at the boy. "I'm sorry."

"If that girl even touches my son again, I will go straight to the police. Do you understand me?"

"Yes, I do," Aunty Mercy says. "I speak English and understand the language very well."

The lady makes a snarly sound, grabs the boy by the arm, and drags him down the front steps and into their car. She squeals her tires and kicks up dust as she leaves, goin' real fast down the road.

Aunty Mercy shut the door. She turned round and lookin' at Felicity, she says "Bib, go up to your room."

"Why? I was colorin'."

"Do as I say."

I go halfway up the stairs and try to hide. Aunt Mercy finds me.

"Go to your room and shut the door." And she waits until I do.

So I don't know nothin' 'bout what they said. When Aunty called me back down, I could tell they'd both been cryin'. Girls cry a lot 'bout near everything. But I ain't never seen Aunty Mercy cry afore.

CHAPTER TEN

Today's New Year's Eve and Stepdaddy's gonna let us stay up right till midnight. Last year, I feel asleep long afore midnight, and did I take a ribbin' from Felicity next mornin'. I woke up on the couch and didn't know where in the world I was. It was kind of a scary feelin'. This year, I reckon if I keep pinching myself, it will keep me awake.

Stepdaddy took me with to go to Piggly Wiggly to buy snacks for the party where we're celebratin'. All the neighbors that'd be there gave a dollar or two to buy snacks for everyone. I got to push the carriage round myself, which Mama never lets me do, 'coz I like to push off with one foot and ride it. She never believes that I'll be careful and not break nothing.

Anyway, I followed him down the aisles as he added things. Everyone had wanted special things and let us know ahead of time. I could see Stepdaddy squintin' at his list. Stepdaddy has a problem readin' his own handwriting. He pushed his cap back a bit.

"What do you think this word is?"

I look at him hopefully. "Cake?"

"No, that can't be. Alva is bringing a cake. Coke? Coca-Cola? No, maybe that's an *r*. Care? Care? That doesn't make sense. Core, apple core. I know no one mentioned they needed coal. Well, isn't this something? How…if only…"

"Let's go onto the next thing, Stepdaddy."

"You're right, son. No use wasting time, if only… Well, never mind. What do we have here? Clips, no chips. Potato chips. Well, now. That's easy."

We go down to the packaged snacks and pick out a big bright blue crinkly bag of chips. It goes into the cart next to some makings for dip and a big bottle of pop.

"Hey, Sam!" We turn round, and one of Stepdaddy's friends from work is there.

"Willy, how are you?" They shake hands and all, Stepdaddy likes meeting people he knows when he's uptown. To my way of thinking, though, he talks an awful long time with 'em.

"Happy New Year, Sam, and to all of the family."

"Thank you, Willy. The same to you, and many more of them. This is my son, Bib. Bib, say hello to Mr. Selter."

"How do you do, Mr. Selter."

"Hello, Bib." Mr. Selter shakes my hand just like if I was a grownup. Then he pretends my handshake hurt so much he had to shake feelin' back into hisself, and I laugh.

"Sam, have you heard about any changes up at the plant?"

"Changes? No, can't say I have."

"No one is talking outright, but the wind's up about something. Hello, Marta. Here comes the wife."

A lady comes walking over. The light above shines on her hair making it gold like a halo. She don't have no angel face, though. She looks sorta mad and tells her husband they gotta go.

And Mr. Selter was none too happy when she just turned round and walked away. He turns and his face is red. "Well, have to go, Sam. We still have a lot of things to do for tonight."

"Of course, Willy. I'll see you back at work."

"Bye, Mr. Selter."

"Happy New Year, Bib," he answers and smiles brighter.

Stepdaddy pauses a while and he's thinking. In the distance, I can hear Mr. and Mrs. Selter arguing. She's saying something about "trailer people," but I can't hear his answer.

"What's next, Stepdaddy?"

"What's that, son? Oh, yes. Let's see. Oranges," he guesses.

After the bus ride home, we go down the dirt road to our trailer carrying all the bags. Felicity helps to put things away, and Mama is full of news.

"Alva is nervous about walking on ice, and I told her you'd help her along, Sam."

"Of course." Alva Kaine is the widder who lives in the trailer on the corner. She only gives out apples at tricks or treats.

"And the Wrights won't be able to make it, little Russell seems to have picked up a bug or something, so Delva doesn't want to risk giving it to the children."

"That's thoughtful. Too many people bring their children out when they're ill. It isn't healthy for anyone, especially the child. We'll save the children some cake, and I'll bring it by tomorrow."

"Thank you, Sam." Mama starts to hum, a sure-fire sign that she's happy. "Bib, if you're going over to have your special party with Miss Alice, you'd better go on and change. It's getting late, and I know Miss Alice has plans for the evening."

"Mama, I changed this mornin' outta my pajamas."

"Morning, Bib."

"Morning, ing, ing, ing." I poke Felicity outta the way of the sink so I can get a glass of water.

"I meant for you to change into your good clothes. Clean underwear, too, mind, and wet your hair a little, it's sticking up in back, and remind me to give your hair a trim before school starts."

I start down the hall, and she's still calling after me to brush my teeth.

It's true. My hair is sticking up in the back. It's dark and curly hair, so it's hard to make it slick down like Jimmy and the other boys in school. I wet my comb and drag it through a few times, but that don't help none. Then I take down the jar of yeller Vaseline and put just a little on that spot, clamp down the comb, and it works just fine. Felicity's knocking on the door and yelling for me to hurry up; she wants to put more junk on her face.

I pretend I can't hear her over the water as I brush my teeth. Then I let her in.

"What's that smell?" she asks.

"What smell?"

"Something smells. What did you put on your hair?"

"Vaseline."

"Vaseline? Oh, for heaven's sake, Bib. You can't put that on your hair."

"Why not? It worked." I leave her to the bathroom and go to change my clothes.

Last year, Miss Alice and her animals gave a little party on New Year's Eve, just for me. I liked it so much that we planned to do it again this year. I dress real careful and remember the underwear.

When Miss Alice opens her door, I can smell her perfume 'coz it's so strong. She has on a pretty, bright orange dress with lots and lots of bead necklaces. I tell her she looks real nice, and she giggles. I never heard Miss Alice giggle afore. Then I see Old Man Johnson sitting on her sofa, and I reckon that she didn't dress up for me. She gives me a big hug and wishes me the happiest New Year ever. I reckon Old Man Johnson is the plan Mama spoke 'bout, and though I like Mr. Johnson, I don't like sharing Miss Alice none.

"Happy New Year, Bib!" he bellows like a cow. In his hand is a Styrofoam cup of something, and he laughs out loud. Miss Alice has a cup too. She giggles again. Dill peeks out from under a rocking chair, and I can tell he's none too pleased neither. I sit down, Dill jumps on my lap, and we share a cup of punch. First I sip, then

Dill. Sometimes, Dill takes longer; sometimes, I do. I reckon it comes out even in the end.

They're both talking and having a grand old time, what with the radio blaring in the background. I never knew they could have so much to talk about. They don't even hear me when I say something. So I sit and glare at Old Mr. Johnson for spoiling my fun. Dill does, too, and I wish I had ears to flatten like he does, 'coz it sure makes a difference.

Finally, Miss Alice remembers I'm there, and she gets me some cookies and tries to talk to me. But she ain't gonna make it up to me that easy. But afore she gets her feelings hurt, I answer her, and we talk a little.

It's just not the same as last year, and I'm kinda sad. I get the feeling they would like me to leave, so they can be alone. I wonder if they's going to get married. That would be awful. Miss Alice said once about a girl her nephew was dating. She said, "I don't understand what in the world they see in one another. So I guess they were made for each other." I feel the same way 'bout Miss Alice and Mr. Johnson. I stand up and thank Miss Alice politely and go to the door. She kisses me and lets me out.

Ahead of me in the cold darkness, I see Mama and Stepdaddy starting out for the Guffman's. The widder Alva is with 'em and so is Mr. and Mrs. Hansen and their kids. I follow them slow, trying to figger out Miss Alice and Mr. Johnson. I wonder if it's something I can ask Mama about or if she'll change the subject on me.

Mr. and Mrs. Guffman's trailer is next to ours. They have four kids, and none of them really play with me, the girls are ten and thirteen and like to be bossed by Felicity. The boys are babies, only four and two. The two-year-old likes to play a game I call "What's that?" which the grownups somehow can ignore, but I gotta play it with him for time on end, and it gets mighty tirin'.

The Guffmans come from Germany, and they have an accent like we do; only theirs is foreign. I like to watch the way their lips and mouth fight each other when they talk English. I heard uptown that the Guffman's were Jews that escaped Germany and came to America after living a few years in England. The people I heard talking said some other things too, and when I told Mama, she covered my lower lip with Ivory Soap.

"Just you remember, Robert, Jesus was Jewish, and so were Joseph and Mary."

I reckon that's when I learned not to repeat things I hear uptown.

Mrs. Guffman is real nice to me and liked it when I helped her plant vegetables in their tiny plot of land, especially later after she showed me which was a weed and which was a carrot top. They don't go to church, they celebrate their Sunday on Friday nights into Saturday, and they do it at home.

Once, they let me stay to supper on their Sabbath night. Everyone was dressed up and clean, and Mrs. Guffman wored a pretty covering over her head and sang to some candles. The songs were such pretty musical language. I sang a song for them from my church and got a big hug for that. They celebrate God real serious-like, but you can tell it makes them happy.

Mr. Guffman is a lot quieter than his wife but likes to smile. He says if someone likes to smile, then they should smile a lot. He reminds me that life is good and how wonderful it is to be alive. I said I guess so, I'd never thought of that much.

On his arm, Mr. Guffman has blue numbers that he can never wash off. Felicity says it's a tattoo, like the man we saw at the carnival, but Mr. Guffman's tattoo was a sad one, so I shouldn't say nothing about it. I don't ever want to make Mr. Guffman so sad that he don't smile or play his fiddle. I can hear his music when I'm lying in bed at night. He plays near every night for his family. I reckon the angels in heaven smile down on Mr. Guffman when they hear his music.

Mama helps Mrs. Guffman pass round some punch to all of us except the babies who fell asleep on the floor covered with blankets. Mr. and Mrs. Jackson are real excited about our new baby coming. They're old retired folks who have grown children living in California. Mr. Jackson worked all his life in the potato factory, and his back is stooped. Mrs. Jackson sometimes takes in sewing work at home. Both of them love children and always get excited when a new baby is borned.

It's midnight. We raise our glasses for a toast. Mr. Guffman makes the first toast, wishing us all long life and happiness in his language. Then he says what he just said in English so's we can understand it.

Stepdaddy gets up and 'coz he likes what he calls ceremony, he bows to everyone. Then he says, "We'll toast to the new year, 1968. May we all live together in peace and harmony, brothers and sisters one to the other."

CHAPTER ELEVEN

When I get to school today, first thing I do is put my composition on Sister's desk. I wanted to get there afore she did, but course, she was already there. She looked at it a little, then thanked me and stuffed it under some other papers on her desk.

Those one hundred words done took me a long time and a lotta thinkin', and it could be treated better than that, to my way of thinkin'. Other kids start coming in, the bell sounding outdoors makes 'em hurry some. I notice that there are a lot of kids absent today, more'n I ever saw in our room. Sister is taking attendance in her black leathery book, once on a while, she glances above her glasses and looks at an empty seat like that very chair has insulted her.

Starting off today, we have geography, which I hate. I can never pronounce those strange names of foreign parts in the world, and I have a lot of trouble remembering where they are, too. I do like to color in the maps and after what seems like a forever lecture on Sister's part about a country called Bolivia; we get the quiet time to mark our maps. We make little crosses where the Sister's Order has missionary stations in the different countries. There ain't many in Bolivia, so I guess they already got God over there.

Jimmy usually sits ahead of me in class, but he's moved to the seat up one, so now an empty desk is between us. He hasn't looked at me once. Worse than that, Sister has noticed and she's treating me nicer than usual. I'm afeared of becoming a teacher's pet.

Right afore recess, Sister Mary Margaret tells us that for our homework we have to write a short essay on the saint we're named for. What that saint stood for, how they died, and how they lived their lives. Stuff like that. Simon Peter is smirking 'coz this is gonna be easy for him. Every kid in this here room could write his essay in ten minutes. When the bells sound for recess, I follow the line outdoors, worrying some 'coz I can't remember if there even was a Saint Robert, never mind what he might have done.

I reckon by Jimmy's reaction to me in class that he's gonna ignore me all day, but he comes over and kicks me saying, "Hey, Bib."

"Hey, Jimmy."

He sits next to me on the ground, and we turn our faces from the wind.

"Didja have a good vacation, Bib?"

"Yeah, it was okay."

"You gonna stay mad at me?"

"Naw. I reckon you gotta do what your folks tell you to do."

"Yeah. My mom likes to lay down the law. I heard my dad say so once. Anyway, she didn't say anything about recess time."

"That's good."

"I know." He's grinning at me, and it makes me realize how much I missed him.

"I'm sorry I missed your birthday. I really wanted to come to your party." Jimmy fishes round in his pocket and brings out a kinda dirty little package. I open it and it's a Superball. Those balls can bounce a mile in the air, if you hit them at the ground hard enough.

"Jeeze, thanks, Jimmy!"

We play with it carefully so's we don't lose it. Jimmy whoops when I got it to go real high.

Sammy White comes to join us, the only boy in the whole school that wears a hat almost the entire year. He takes a lot of kidding, but he don't care. His mama makes him wear it whether he wants to or not. She's another mama what likes to lay down the law. Sammy gets earaches all year long. She's tired of him being sick so much. She says the hat will keep his ears warm, the germs away, and Sammy from out under her feet.

"Say, guys, do ya think there's a Saint Sammy?"

"You mean Samuel, you knucklehead," says Jimmy, but not in a mean way. "Course there is. It's a Bible name."

"Good. I don't want to have to use my middle name." Sammy and us sit down and start throwing pieces of ice to scare the group of girls across the way. They just ignore us though.

"What's your middle name?" I ask.

"Never mind, Saint Bib."

"I was named for Saint James the Dismembered," Jimmy says, lying. He's been fixed on that saint ever since we read about him in *The Golden Legends*. His eyes light up, and I can see him starting to think on all the gory details he could write to make Sister mad. Gentle Jimmy, who cried over a dead bird we found by Lark's Pond makin' me swear never to tell no one. He likes stories about battles and bloody martyr deaths.

"Naw, you weren't. You were named for St. James the Greater."

"Oh yeah? How would you know?"

"Simple," says Sammy. "Your mom told my mom."

"Oh."

"Well, I'm gonna write 'bout St. Francis. He's my favorite, and that's my middle name anyway," I decide.

"You're lucky. There's lots of books on him."

"Not as lucky as Simon Peter. He'll have his done afore he leaves school today."

We all think on the luck some kids have when their parents name them. It just don't seem fair.

After supper, it's my turn to clear the table. I spose it's better than washin' dishes, but it ain't easy 'coz there's hardly enough counter space. Then I take out my notebook to write another composition. Mama sits next to me and tells me stories about St. Francis, how he tamed a wolf, and how the birds used to quiet down and listen to him talk.

"St. Francis was a gentle man who loved all living things," says Mama. "People, animals, the sick and the poor. All of them with an equal love he gave to God himself. We could use another St. Francis in the world today."

"We sure could." Stepdaddy is sitting and reading the newspaper. Lately, he's been looking worrieder and worrieder.

"Someone's knocking at the front door," Felicity says over the television. When Mama and Stepdaddy gave Felicity permission to watch that there rock group The Rolling Stones on Ed Sullivan a year ago, Felicity has acted high and mighty over the television. She's not sposed to be watching it now, she's sposed to be doin' her homework.

"Shut that off, Felicity, and do your homework." Mama finally noticed her.

Stepdaddy opens the door. "Mr. Alderson. Good evening. Come on in, we've got the coffee pot on, and I'm sure you would like a cup after being out in this cold."

"Thank you, Mr. Harper, but I can only stay a moment."

"Won't take a moment." Mama smiles at him and goes to pour him a cup.

I guess Mr. Alderson can't decide what to do. He keeps looking at the chair, then at Mama, and at the chair again. He sits down.

"What brings you out this evening Mr. Alderson?"

He takes a sip of coffee. "I always did say, Mrs. Harper, you make the best coffee around."

"Thank you."

Mama's clearly surprised at this here visit. Mr. Alderson is our landlord. He owns all the trailers 'cept Miss Alice's, and we never see him round much, 'coz Stepdaddy mails him the rent check to his big house uptown.

Mr. Alderson clears his throat like he's gonna say somethin', then seems to change his mind as he takes a sip of coffee. He starts to tap his foot on the floor under the table. I can tell 'coz he's sitting next to me.

"Well, Mr. and Mrs. Harper, I'm afraid I haven't come here for a social call. I've been seeing all the folks at the park to let them know that beginning on March first, I'm going to have to raise the rents."

"I see," Stepdaddy says.

Mr. Alderson looks away from Stepdaddy. He's concentrating on the china plates lined up on the wall shelf. "I'm truly sorry about this, Mr. Harper."

"I imagine you are, Mr. Alderson." Mama's voice sounds strange when she says this.

"You don't have to explain, nor apologize, Mr. Alderson. Claire and I know what the bottom line means to the businessman."

"Well, I wouldn't put it that way—"

Stepdaddy interrupts him. His eyes are stormy mad. "Just tell us how much you are raising the rent, Mr. Alderson. We won't waste any time, you and I, over the hows and whys. I'm sure that the increase will be a fair one."

Mr. Alderson looks away again at the china he seems to like so much. "It will be another ten dollars a week, Mr. Harper."

"Ten dollars...a week? Surely you don't mean every week, Mr. Alderson. That's forty dollars a month." Mama's hand shakes as she clutches the cream pitcher.

"As, I said, I am sorry, Mrs. Harper, but I'm afraid it is necessary."

"Forty dollars a month?" Mama asks again.

"A very nice and steady profit for you, Mr. Alderson. With seven trailers that would be two hundred and eighty dollars more in your pocket each month. I hadn't realized that property taxes in Crystal Springs had risen so high." Stepdaddy has a sort of controlled anger about him now, much scarier than if he's yelling and hittin' the ceiling. Felicity comes to stand behind me and puts her hand tucked between my back and the chair. Her hand is shaking just like Mama's.

Mr. Alderson stands up and buttons his coat. "I'm sorry you feel the need to use sarcasm, Harper. Better than a downright fight, I guess, but not as satisfactory."

Stepdaddy stands up. He's inches higher than Mr. Alderson, and you can hardly see the landlord because of the width of Stepdaddy's shoulders. "We have been living here for nearly three years, Alderson, and never a complaint from you. I believe I have even heard you mention once or twice that we are model tenants."

Mr. Alderson looks a little sad, but maybe it's the light 'coz he looks mean soon after. He says nothing until he opens the door. "March first, Harper." And he's gone.

Stepdaddy stares out the window watchin' the landlord walk down the road. Behind him, Mama starts to cry. I haven't heard Mama cry for I don't know how long. Of all of us, she's the one who never seemed to be sad or worry. And for once, Stepdaddy don't come over to put his arms round her to comfort her. He's just standing at the window, his shoulders drooping.

I stuff my St. Francis paper into my notebook, and Felicity and me leave them alone. We get up to get ready for bed without being asked.

CHAPTER TWELVE

Stepdaddy don't eat with us anymore in the mornings. He's puttin' in overtime at the potato plant since they cut his pay.

Mama isn't like Mama anymore. She stares into space a lot and traces the beads of her rosary without even praying. Felicity's been going to school, but Mama has had me stay home this last week since the landlord came to see us. I sure don't miss school that much, but it was a lot easier than staying home 'coz Mama gives me even harder lessons to work on than Sister Mary Margaret. And I have to keep up at school. Felicity brings my homework home. To my way of thinkin', it's gonna be impossible to keep both of them happy. I gotta work every morning right after breakfast. All day long, all I hear is Mama correcting my English. Once she said she's tired of listenin' to me soundin' like an ignorant Southerner. Mama don't ever insult us. My eyes stung just a little bit when she said it. So I'm tryin' real hard to sound just as educated as Stepdaddy.

This morning, Felicity made the oatmeal and set down a glass of milk for Mama. She didn't really see it, and Felicity reminds her to eat and drink. "Think of the baby," Felicity says, so Mama eats.

When Felicity left for school, and as I got out my school books, we were surprised by a visit from Father John.

"Well, Bib! What a blessed morning indeed. The sun is shining, and the birds are planning on their trip home to live among us." He gives my shoulders a big squeeze and smiles at Mama. "Good morning, Claire."

"Father John. What brings you out this way?"

"Well, now, I'll be telling you." Father takes off his overcoat and his muffler and hands them to me. "Whilst I was traveling down by this bit of road, I was after thinking to meself, now which parishioner lives down this way willing to visit with an old man like meself, and her with the percolator a-goin'?"

I hear Mama laughing for the first time this week, and she hands Father a steaming cup of coffee in one of our good cups without one chip in it. Father settles down into a chair at the table with a sigh and looks at his feet with a sad face.

"Claire, I amn't not as young as I was, and I'm not one to give out. But sure me feet are telling me so. I can remember I could walk four miles on a Sunday, after a delicious dinner cooked by my blessed mammy, God rest her soul."

"God rest her soul," we echo.

"And himself, me Da, trying to keep up and me laughing. He told me that one day I would be old too, and my feet are after telling me so."

"Maybe your shoes are too tight, Father."

"Just so, Bib, you may be right. Now, go along with you like a good lad and let me have a few words alone with your mammy."

I walk down the hallway, and when they're not looking, I turn round and sneak back, crawling, until I can hide behind the upholstered rocking chair. I'm not sure eavesdropping is a sin. It probably is, so I reckon I'll be confessing it on Saturday.

First, they're quiet and sipping their coffee. I peek and see Mama isn't making happy little comments like she usually does, and she don't look up from her coffee too much.

"Well, Claire dear, and I can see it's no use for small talk this morning. I have heard about the troubles you be having, and the others too, of course, in the park."

"Word gets around fast, Father."

"Aye, in Crystal Springs the grapevine is as busy as any a village back home. In case you're wondering, 'twas me own housekeeper, Mrs. Baker, what told me, and a more caring woman never lived."

"Yes, Father, Mrs. Baker is a fine woman. You are in good hands with Mrs. Baker taking care of you."

"Good hands, Claire, and a mighty tongue as well."

Mama fills the coffee cups again. I can hear the clink of the metal pot against the china.

"Claire, I've come today, not only as your priest, but as your friend. Many a time we can be using a helping hand to follow up our prayers in this world. I don't have to tell you that I'm praying for you all. And the Good

Lord will answer me prayer, I know, and come to your aid. But I'll want you to have this as well."

"Father, I will accept your prayers with a grateful heart, but we will not take charity."

"'Tis not charity I be offering. Only a bit to tide you over."

"There are many, many needy families in your parish. There are people without food to eat tonight. My family will eat tonight, tomorrow, and the next day. And, may it please the Lord, we will have a roof over our heads for many days to come."

"'Tis true, what you say, Claire. There be no use arguing with you."

I can see Mama smiling, and she offers Father John a piece of date bread she baked yesterday.

"Ah, Claire, if I weren't a priest, sure I would be holed up in a nice quiet monastery somewhere in me beautiful Ireland with only stone walls and roses around me, and me and God conversing."

"You love people too much for that, Father."

"Ah, 'tis true. I love the people here. And, of course, Minnesota is beautiful in itself. Yes, it'll do. Not as beautiful as Ireland, mind, but it'll do. And all the lads and lasses. Little Bib, such a fine young lad is he, smart as they come. I'm hearing he's doing very well in school."

Mama doesn't say anything for a minute.

"Poor wee lad. It is sad, indeed, when a wee one gets sick this time of year. But I'm sure he'll be fit and fine on Monday next."

"Yes, Father. I think Bib will be able to go back to school Monday."

"Good, good. Splendid. Now, me dear, I must be going. I'm after going to see me bishop, and need I be telling you the honest truth, I amn't looking forward to it. But even priests have to share their troubles with someone now and then, not God alone."

"Troubles? Whatever is the matter, Father?"

"Well, now, wouldn't it be easy just to kneel in front of the Blessed Sacrament and pray the day away. But we priests, as you know, are blessed in our giving of help in other ways too. Sure 'tis a fine feeling to know you've helped a parishioner in need, and heaven will bless you as you do. But, oh, when the parish no longer needs your helping hand." Father sighed and looked sadly at his coffee.

"Father Patrick O'Rourke, you are a crafty man."

"Ah, and didn't me mammy be telling me so many a time when I was a lad."

"Yes, and your blessed mother, God rest her soul, must have achieved her sainthood after raising you."

"Not a minute in purgatory did she spend after raising a fine lot of God-fearing lads."

There was a long silence, and I could see Mama and Father John looking at each other.

"Tell me, Father, would it be possible for St. Francis to lend some money to our family to tide us over in our hour of need?" Mama says, smiling.

"'Tis a wonderful idea, that, Claire. And wouldn't we be twice blessed to do so?" Father is smiling like a little boy and even claps his hands once.

"Now here you are, a loan as you say, and we be expecting it back sometime in the future. Now off I must go."

"To see the bishop?" Mama said in a teasing way.

"Bishop? I see no reason to be botherin' the bishop this day, and him being such a busy man." He raised his voice to me. "And Bib, an Act of Contrition from you, me lad, after telling your ten Our Fathers for eavesdropping."

"Yes, Father," I said it behind the chair, and then I stood up since they knew I was there.

Mama helps him on with his overcoat and winds the muffler round his neck. Father lifts a hand and cups her cheek for a moment. Then he raises his gentle hand and blesses us and our home as we kneel in front of him. I see the picture of the Sacred Heart of Jesus afore me on the wall, and peace seems to shine from it and beside me Mama is more relaxed than she's been for some time.

Then Father adds a little something of his own. He looks into Mama's eyes and says, "'As for me and my house, we will serve the Lord.'"

CHAPTER THIRTEEN

When Stepdaddy came home from work covered with potato dirt, he was sure surprised at the fifty-dollar bill that Mama showed him. After she told him about Father John's visit and all, he had to sit down he was laughing so hard.

"The Lord is certainly lucky that Father John is on His side rather than the devil. Father could talk Satan himself into salvation."

"You're right, Sam. And you were right about Bib being out of school too. Father let me know that, in his own way of course. Bib will be back to school on Monday."

Stepdaddy pulled Mama into his lap. "I knew you would have him go back, either way, Claire. You're too smart to let other's ignorance stand in our way. You reacted in fear, and no one would hold that against you when it comes to your children. Many people would have reacted much worse. You were only protecting your young."

I watch from the sofa as Mama hides her face in Stepdaddy's shoulder, and he rocks her back and forth like a little baby.

"What are we going to do?" she asks his shoulder.

"What we've always done. Go on. No one can really hurt us except ourselves. The worst injury we could cause ourselves would be to give up. We'll stand up against the world, shout from the roof tops, and rattle our very bones until we're heard. Now listen, Claire." He pulls her round gently until they are face to face. "We don't have a large army with which to fight, but we have our family and our neighbors in this park. We've decided to meet and talk over the best strategy to handle this. I don't understand how this can be legal, this move to raise our rents so high. It must be political, coming from the town hall. You know what they said on the radio about the recent trouble across the country—"

"Hush, Sam, Bib's in the room."

Stepdaddy looks at me. "Yes, Bib's in the room. He's only nine, a child that should be playing in the sun. But he will have to grow up faster than we'd like him to, Claire. We both know it's time. We have a hard fight ahead of us."

"Yes, Sam. I know. I've been hoping it wouldn't come to this, that we had found a safe place in this far away town. I don't know why, but I thought we could run from everything and be a happy family here in Crystal Springs. It seemed like such a wonderful little town."

"But you are right, Claire. It is a wonderful little town, and we'll see it that way again. Nothing lasts forever, as that old adage claims. We are happy. We will remain happy together. Nothing can change that. Tonight, we'll be meeting in Mr. Johnson's trailer. He doesn't want to worry Miss Alice, so no one has approached her about this yet. After supper, Felicity will have to help Olive Guffman to babysit all of the children as we meet."

"Felicity won't like that, Stepdaddy," I say.

"That's true, son, but this is not the time for us to sit back and do as we please. Well, I'm off to shower and perhaps get a few minutes of sleep. Will you wake me up at five, Claire?"

"Yes." She kisses him afore he goes.

"Bib, you watch things here will I go over to speak to Mrs. Guffman."

"Yes, Mama."

"Read your book and no running around."

"Yes, Mama." Mamas may forgive bad things you've done, but they never forget them.

I can hear the crunch of her footsteps as she walks over the snow to go next door. The sound of the shower is somehow comforting, like rain in the springtime what feeds the flowers. I feel cozy and warm next to the stove on the sofa, and I lie down all covered up with the afghan. I like to read, like to get lost in the pages. This week, I got a good book out of the liberry, *Stuart Little*, and I can hardly wait to go back reading it. I took the book out myself with my own liberry card. Once, I was too lazy to go with Mama and asked her to get a book for me. She picked out The Bobbsey Twins, and I will sure never ask her again.

Round about three o'clock, Mama's not home yet, and Stepdaddy's asleep. Felicity walks through the door home from school, dumps her books all over the sofa, and takes off her coat so she can hang it up.

"How is Your Highness today? Enjoy another day off from school?"

"Yes, ma'am, sure did."

"You beat all, you know that? Mama's precious baby you are. Well, wait until the new baby is born. Then you'll see." She pushes my legs offa the sofa and sits down.

"See what?"

"What it's like not to be the precious baby. Where's Mother?"

"Next door at the Guffman's. There's gonna be a meeting tonight with all the neighbors, 'cept for the kids, and you and Olive have to babysit every single kid in this here park all by yourselves. Even the babies that need their diapers changed."

"Who told you that?" she demanded.

"Stepdaddy."

"What are they meeting about that's so important that I have to watch a bunch of kids?"

"Stepdaddy says all the grownups are going to figger out how to fight the landlord."

"Oh." She is thinking to herself as she picks up her scattered books. I know the look on her face when she's thinking. When Felicity thinks, her eyes kinda blurr and she don't notice anythin' goin' on round her. Once, when she was in a thinkin' mood, I put popcorn in her hair and she never did notice. Of a sudden it's awful quiet and serious in the room.

"Babies, babies, smelly old diaper babies!" I make a song out of it. But she don't even hear me. "Felicity? Aren't you mad?"

"No, Bib. I hate to spoil this for you, but this time, I'm not mad." And she just leaves with her books to our bedroom.

Later, we eat supper a lot faster than we usually do. Mama even puts the dishes in the sink to soak without washing them. This is something I've never seen her do afore in all my life. It makes me reckon that what's going on is a lot more important than I thought. She hurries us along to put on our coats.

Outside, Felicity turns right to go to the Guffman's. I stay with Mama and Stepdaddy and turn left toward Old Mr. Johnson's trailer.

"Bib." Mama stops. "Go with Felicity."

"No."

"Bib, do as your Mama says."

"No." I dig my feet into the snow and look at them both without even being scared, even though I never done told them no like this afore.

"Robert Francis—"

"Wait, Claire," Stepdaddy interrupts. "Let's hear his explanation of why he is acting this way." He gets down on one knee and looks me in the face. "Bib, we have something very important to attend to tonight, and you know your Mama and I need you to behave."

"I know."

"Then why aren't you minding us?"

"Because," I say to him, "because, Daddy, I'm gonna be a soldier in your army."

Mama and Daddy look at each other for what seems a long time. Then they just start walking again with me trailing behind.

Mr. Johnson's trailer is packed with all the grownups in the park. There's hardly no place to sit, but Mr. Johnson puts me in a tight corner out of the way. He don't seem too surprised to see me there. No one does. The talk is going on something fierce. Everyone is scared, everyone is mad. Widder Alva Kaine is shivering next to me, and Mama brings her a shawl and holds her hand talking gentle-like. I hold her other hand, and she squeezes it.

When everyone gets their madness offa their chests, Old Mr. Johnson begins. "Well, we all know why we're here. We've all had a recent visit from Mr. Alderson to let us know that we will be paying more, much more, for the privilege of living in his trailers. I talked this morning to Lawyer Banyon. He told me that with the town involved as it is, and the current emotions across this town right now, there isn't a lawyer in the county who would touch this with a ten foot pole."

"But this is a legal fight," Daddy says.

"Not legal for us, Sam. Alderson owns this property, and he can do what he wants with it. My guess is that it isn't a personal issue with him, purely financial. He's most likely been offered a hunk of change he can't refuse. Now, we've all signed leases that don't run out until next January. That's the way he worked, our leases begin and end in January. But the town don't want to wait until next year to get us out. He can't refuse to renew all of our leases at one time. So he raises our rent, which he can do legally since he's given us notice, and when we can't afford to stay, we leave and he has a somewhat clear conscience."

"Then what can we do?" Mr. Wright speaks up. Mr. Wright lives in the yeller trailer right at the beginning of our road. He lives there with Mrs. Wright ('coz she's his wife), and three kids who are all way younger 'n me and real bratty to my way of thinkin'. They never do what their mama tells 'em to. They yell and scream and play inna mud so they always got dirty faces and clothes. Mama clucks her tongue when she sees them on the street. I know she's thinkin' that soap don't cost much and our water is free, coz I've heard her say that time and again. But I think Mrs. Wright is just plumb wored out. "You say we have no legal stand. I have three children to feed. Where can we go? The Missus has checked the paper. There isn't a rental property within ten miles of Crystal Springs."

"Exactly."

"What do you mean *exactly*?" Mama asks.

Mr. Johnson looks round the room. "The town wants us out. Not only out of the trailer park, but out of Crystal Springs entirely. I've seen it coming for a long time. Look at what we're sitting on. This piece of property is on the bus line and on Route 113 that follows to the center of town. It's adjacent to the church and the school. Development here would mean money in every grubby fist from the mayor on down to the contractors and new store owners will locate here. People in this town won't care that they're throwing seven families out into the streets. We're different and expendable because we're people who are poor, retired or living on Social Security. We mind our own business. We're good people, kind people. But the town don't know that. They just see us as an obstacle to their plans."

Widder Alva starts to cry. That makes me feel awful bad, 'coz Widder Alva is so tiny and helpless like a little bunny. She has so many wrinkles she looks like a walnut. Her clothes are walnut-colored, too. She don't make any noise when she cries; the tears just run down her cheek real slow, slow, slow. I dunno why, but it makes her seem sadder cryin' like that.

"What can we do?" The cries from the people fly up into the stuffy air of the trailer and bounces off the ceiling.

Suddenly, there's a banging at the door. Not a knock, a full-fist banging that makes the door shudder with hurt.

"The landlord," I whisper, and Widder Alva begins to shake again.

"Let me in, Johnson, you old sod!"

Mr. Johnson opens the door, and Miss Alice stalks into the room like a mad rooster. Dill follows her, swishing his tail back and forth.

"Alice—"

"Don't 'Alice' me, you old fool. Don't you think I know what's going on around here? Think I have my head in the sand? Think I don't understand English?"

"I didn't think—"

"That's your problem, old man, you don't think. You don't use your fool head for nothin' but to keep your ears in place. Now you," she says, and it's like she sees all our faces in one. "What are you doing, having a meeting without telling me? What were you going to do, slink out in the middle of the night, and leave me alone in this godforsaken place?"

"I'm sorry, Miss Alice," Daddy tells her. "I just thought—"

"That's your problem, Sam Harper, you think too much."

"We didn't want to worry you," Daddy said.

"Worry. Humph. Worry. I have no worries. You have worries. Do you come to me about your worries? No. You go to this old fool here." She points her thumb at Mr. Johnson. "Well, let me tell you a thing or two. This town may want a new fancy shopping center, but they won't get it."

"What do you mean?"

"Jesus, Mary, and Joseph, help me! Who owns the largest piece of property in this park? I'm not talking about the little squats you're renting. I'm talking about my property, which extends into the woods and runs right along Rte 113, which they need for a right of way access. Even the bit of road you walk every day."

There's a silence in the room. Miss Alice in this mood is a stronger force than the tornadoes that pass over us. "I do! I own it, and I'm not selling!" She turns round, calls Mr. Johnson an old fool again, and she and Dill go out, slamming the door behind them.

Then I remember the deed she likes to show me with the fancy signings' on the bottom.

CHAPTER FOURTEEN

February vacation is here, one whole week off of school, and I gotta work on stuff left over from when Mama kept me out of school. Anyway, the weather's warmer, and I can go sledding or out to play after breakfast and do my homework at night.

Cannon Weight went sledding with me a few times. He likes to fall over and bury his nose in the snow. Then he shakes his head, scattering the snow in all directions and grins. Since this is his favorite part, it's hard to make the slide all the way down the hill. He moves his rump just as we start to round the tough corner, and we spill over on the bank. This afternoon, he took off with my hat, becoming bored with sliding and all and deciding to play keep-away.

I had a mighty hard time catching up to him what with I had to drag my sled behind me. I swear Cannon Weight had that hat chomped right down his throat. We wrestled a good bit till he finally let go, leaving me on my back in the street. He must have smelled his lunch because he nudged me along. Cannon Weight is not one to miss lunch.

Miss Alice met us at the door and asked if we left any snow on the hill at all. She helped me out of all my outer clothes and even helped to pull off my boots that get stuck, even wearing plastic bags. We got 'em off, and Cannon Weight went into the kitchen and sat to wait patient-like until Dill finished eating. Dill won't ever let anyone eat afore him.

"Bib, how would you like a nice bowl of hot soup?"

"Yes, ma'am, I'd like that a real lot."

"Well, pull up to the table, honey. I ain't no waitress serving soup in my living room."

We both sat down, and she gave me a huge spoon, what she calls a soup spoon, and I can hardly fit the thing in my mouth. She also gives me some oyster crackers, little tiny light things that are crispy, but you have to have a mouthful to get even a taste. I like to float them in the soup, holding them captive under the hot broth until they swell up and get soft.

"Did I tell you about Little Alice, Bib?"

I perk up my ears. "No." Little Alice is Miss Alice's grand niece, and she's always getting into some trouble or other. I love Little Alice stories, so I sit up straight and eat as quiet as I can so the new story won't get interrupted.

"Little Alice, heaven's sake, the girl has no brains at all. I swear to you, Bib, she goes to the city, not St. Cloud, of course, where you can at least get a good meal for under a dollar, but Minneapolis! Minneapolis without hide nor hair of support, expecting to find a job just like that. No place to live, no friends, no relations except my cousin Raymond who's as useless as the day is long, and just as boring, and there she is in the middle of a city of concrete, wandering the streets, knocking on doors looking for work. Strangers' doors! I never heard the like. That's what I told her grandmother, my sister Caroline, I said, 'I never heard the like of your grandbaby, Little Alice, Caroline.' She agreed with me even though it's her own grandbaby, we all know the girl was born wantin'. Anyway, there was Little Alice sitting on a park bench, but not in a park, they have no such things as parks in Minneapolis, I'm told, because nothing grows from concrete, but she sat on a bench outside of a fancy restaurant and suddenly, out of nowhere, a man approaches her! Now, of course her grandmother, my sister Caroline, we both told Little Alice what to do if a stranger tries to talk to her. Heaven's sake, we've been telling her since she was three! But you know, Little Alice is now twenty and of course she knows everything. Everything, she thinks, even when she doesn't have a lick of sense in her. She's got her guitar with her and the man asks her if she sings, she says yes, and right there on the street she opens up the case, takes out the guitar and starts singing one of those whiny songs you hear on the radio nowadays. You know, the songs where you can't even understand the words. Why write a song when you can't understand it? Anyway, Bib, you know the shame in something like that, I told my sister Caroline so. Singing like a beggar in the middle of the city. Anyway, turns out the man was someone important in that fancy restaurant and offered her a job, just like that. Now she's staying with Cousin Raymond until she finds her own place to live."

Miss Alice looks at me real stern, almost like Sister Mary Margaret. "So now you see, Bib. You never talk to strangers."

"But, Miss Alice, if Little Alice hadn't talked to that stranger man, she wouldn't have got a job."

"That's the point right there! Who is this man? Do we know? Does Little Alice know? Of course not. Do you know how long it takes to know someone? A long time, I'm telling you, and now here's poor Little Alice at the mercy of a strange man in the middle of that dratted city that's more concrete than human."

I wonder about Miss Alice sometimes.

While we're talking, I hear a mighty bang on the door, and right away, Cannon Weight starts to bark. He runs to the door, snuffing under it and a deep growl starts in the back of his throat. I've never heard him do such a thing.

"Quiet!" One word from Miss Alice, and Cannon Weight slinks into the background but not too far away. He hides and peeks round the archway that leads to the hall.

Out on the stoop, I see two men in suits and overcoats. One of them looks like the angry bald man I saw in the pickup truck I saw a long time ago.

"What do you want?" Miss Alice is not using her company voice.

"Miss Batchelder?" The man with hair gives her a big smile.

"That's me. What do you want?"

"May we come inside, ma'am?"

"What for?"

"We'd like to talk to you about a business proposition, Miss Batchelder. If you can see your way clear to give us a few moments of your time, I'm sure we can make it worth your while."

"Business? I have no business with you. Don't even know you. As for time, my time's my own business and worth plenty already, I can tell you."

The man continues to smile, but it's almost slipped offa his face. He tries again. "Miss Batchelder, we represent Farmer's Developing Company. Perhaps you've heard of us?"

"Developers, huh?"

"Yes, ma'am."

"Never heard of you. Don't know what good you can do me, but come in anyhow."

Miss Alice steps aside and lets the men in the room. She nods over to the table where I'm sitting and says, "Sit there."

The man with the hair places his briefcase right next to my bowl of soup, which I ain't even done with yet. He looks at me real close.

"Your little boy, ma'am?"

She hoots. "That's Bib. Lives across the way."

"Perhaps he's a little young to be included in this conversation?"

"Well, I figure Bib has more right to stay than you, considering he was invited."

You can tell both men are getting mighty frustrated, but they're trying not to show it. They smile at me as if they liked me and said hi, but I just keep on eating my soup. I know if I pretend like I'm not listening, they'll talk more.

Miss Alice isn't patient at all. "Well?"

"Miss Batchelder, we represent the—"

"You already told me that. I am old. I am cross. But I ain't deaf and I ain't blind. You're here representing those snakes from the city. Why can't you just come out and say that? What's the use of empty words, just take up space in your ear. Well, how much?"

The bald man speaks up. "I can assure you, ma'am, that our company is prepared to make an offer to you that is extremely generous and more than fair."

"Well, I'm sure they'll make an offer, but I'm equally sure they're not fair. Go on."

"The Farmer's Development Company will pay you five thousand dollars for your property." Both men smile at Miss Alice and look very satisfied with theirselves.

"Five thousand dollars, huh? You out of your minds? What do you think this is, Rockerfeller's Mansion? If your company is willing to spend that much on this bitty piece of land, then you have to be more rotten than I thought. And so are those bigwigs you're representing, and the bigwigs they're representing. Five thousand dollars. I feel sorry for men like you, thinking the whole world is for sale and the people in it."

"Now look here, Miss Batchelder—"

"No. You look. Take a good look as you walk out my door. Now."

Miss Alice gets up and walks to the door, graceful as a queen, with her head held high just like Mama does. Bald man slams his briefcase and both of them hurry out the door. Miss Alice bangs the door shut, and Cannon Weight comes over to lick her hand.

"Bib, don't tell your Mama I told you this, but sometimes, there's no purer satisfaction than slamming a door."

"Miss Alice, five thousand dollars! You'd be rich."

"Robert Francis Harper. You've lost your mind, filling your head with dollar signs. Stop it this minute, do you hear? Can paradise be bought?"

"No."

"Right. Heaven's sake. This here land, this is my own piece of property, owned by my family for I don't know how long. I'm too angry to remember. Generations, anyway. We used to share crop, even here in Minnesota the farmers would take advantage of season workers. My family would help with the cornstalks from dawn until after suppertime. And they saved every penny they could to buy themselves a place they could call own. And this is it. If you compare five thousand dollars to the pleasure of being able to do what you want on your own land, those dollars shrink in comparison."

"Yes, ma'am."

"Bib, my little friend, you say yes ma'am and agree with what I say with your polite little mouth, but not your intelligent mind. You're just too young to see the injustice around you." She comes over and puts her thin arms round me and gives me a big squeeze.

CHAPTER FIFTEEN

That night, and the next night too, I had real trouble sleeping. Those two men who I never even learned their names, they kept haunting me. When I close my eyes, I see the bald man get angrier and angrier, redder and redder in the face. He's screaming out words I don't understand.

Mama's been wondering that I ain't sleeping, but I tell her I'm fine. I know what those men are about, and they will cause Mama and Daddy to worry even more. I don't usually keep secrets very well, but I keep this one, and it gets heavier inside me every day.

Tonight, there's another of those great winds whipping through the park, not a tornado, but like a little tornado child. There's an oak tree between our yard and the Guffman's with long branches that stretch over our roof. Those branches keep tapping and knocking, sounding like something scary wanting to get in. Once I slipped out of bed to go to Mama, but after I see they're both so sound asleep and comfortable, I go back to my own bed which has grown cold because I forgot and left the covers down. Even Felicity is sleeping.

So I guess that as Mama says, my imagination is working overtime again. Because in the night sounds, I seem to hear footsteps and talking and wood breaking. And rap, rap on the ceiling over my head. Sounds that mix together and become so terrible that I know if someone did come to my door, I'd be too afeared to scream. I sure wish Dill was with me. Next to my bed is my little desk, and I risk everything to get to it and get my old Winnie the Pooh bear from when I was little. I hug him tight and pull the covers over both our heads. That doesn't work very well, because if you can't see nothing, even shadows in the room, you see worse things in your mind under the covers. So we lay there with our heads out, Winnie and I, until the sky begins to break apart, darkness and then light. Out the window, I see the lightness getting stronger and becoming a pale pink. That's when I finally fall asleep.

Mama comes in to wake me for breakfast. She looks so unhappy that I know right away those night sounds were real. I know enough not to ask what's wrong yet. She takes Winnie from me and asks, "Didn't sleep well, Bib?"

"No, Mama. I heard things. Awful scary things."

She scoops me out of bed and I'm on her lap. "Why didn't you wake me?"

"I don't know, Mama."

"Come and eat your breakfast. Then we're all going to get together to help."

I have to find my slippers that went under the bed and I look up at her. "Help with what?"

Mama sighs as if she's very, very tired. "You'll see. Come and eat your breakfast."

I see that Felicity is out of bed ahead of me, something that hardly ever happens.

At the table, we drink our juice, and Daddy is standing at the door again, looking out and not even noticing that the steam of his coffee cup seems to be hurting his eyes, 'coz his eyes are watering. I try to see outside, but he puts out an arm to stop me.

"Wait," is all he says.

Felicity is quiet and picking at her eggs. She breaks the yolks and they flood and swirl round her plate. Mama usually gets upset if we play with our food, but this time, she watches Felicity and don't say nothing. Mama is holding her teacup so hard, her knuckles are white. This morning, I noticed that Mama's body is changing, her tummy is sticking out more. I know my baby brother is in that tummy, Jimmy told me so once, and now I'm wondering how he can breathe in there. Maybe he has gills, like a fish. I think of asking, but change my mind. The air in here is too heavy.

Felicity gets up and clears the table. She's done already dressed. I go to get dressed too, and we all put on our coats and go outside. And what I see I can hardly believe.

At first, I thought that the little tornado child last night had become a grownup tornado. But then, everywhere I look, it's just pure destruction. Like on some news shows we see afore Mama shuts the television off.

Mama's little willer tree out front has been pulled up; its naked branches are stretching out and up into the cold. Her flower beds have been dug into; the little bulbs inside won't be coming up again. The oak tree has been scarred with knives and hatchets, exposing the tree so much I wonder if it will die. And dirty words have been painted all over the front of our trailer that Mama tries to keep so nice and clean.

The Guffman family is in front of their own trailer. Mrs. Guffman is crying real hard, and Daddy goes over to be with them; then we all go over. When I look up, I see that their trailer is full of paint, red funny pointed stars and ugly evil black crosses with tips on the ends. Those crosses look like angry black spiders. I don't know why, but for some reason they scare me.

Mrs. Guffman is crying. "It is happening, Isaac, all over again. It is happening."

And Mr. Guffman is hugging her, saying, "No, no, Rebecca, it is not happening all over again. This is America. This is America. It cannot be happening all over again."

I run over to Miss Alice. Her mesh fence is cut with great gashes. Her yard looks like it's been bombed with Fourth of July cherry bombs. Every bush is dug up, lying like dead things in the snow. I rush up the step and bang on her door. I can see the door is all twisted and doesn't close right.

"Miss Alice! Miss Alice!" I scream and begin to cry.

Then I hear her footprints and her door opens a crack. One eye is looking at me.

"Miss Alice, let me in please."

"Bib, I'm okay. Don't cry. Please go get your daddy."

"What's wrong with you? Where are Dill and Tom?"

"I'm okay, the animals are fine. Get your daddy, now." Her voice is hoarse and gasping.

I turn and run as fast as I can, screaming for Mama and Daddy. Then they run with me, and Daddy forces the door without even knocking.

Miss Alice is sitting on her sofa, and it don't look like Miss Alice, not at all. Her head is covered with blood, one eye is swelled shut and bruised black. When she opens her mouth, I can see her gums are bloody too. Mama makes her lay down and tells me to find a blanket to cover her. The whole trailer is a mess, smashed mirrors, slivers of glass everywhere. Clothes have been thrown round, and every family picture Miss Alice has is smashed. But her family keeps smiling through the cracked glass. Finally, I find a blanket and run back into the living room. Daddy tried to call an ambulance, but he said the phone lines had been cut. So he ran to Mr. Johnson to ask him to drive uptown for help.

Gently, Mama lays Miss Alice's arm across her chest, and I feel sick when I can see the bone through her flesh.

"Bib, get a cloth and some warm water."

I go into the kitchen, and the same thing has happened there. Destruction and hate. I can feel it. Dill is sitting on the counter and Cannon Weight is hiding under the table. I don't have time to look for Tom. I pour warm water in the first bowl I see and take it and a cloth back to Mama.

"You too?" Miss Alice whispers.

"Hush, Miss Alice. Hush now and rest. Sam is getting help for you. Don't you worry about us."

Tears slide down Miss Alice's cheeks, leaving little paths wherever they go. Dill has come to sit next to her, protecting her. I pet him, and he purrs a little to let me know that he knows I'm there, but then, his attention is set back on Miss Alice.

"I wouldn't let them in," she whispers. "I wouldn't let them in."

"Sshh."

"I wouldn't let them in," she whispers again and closes her eyes. I'm afeared she's dead, but Mama hushes me and says Miss Alice will be fine.

Outside, we hear a car pull up, and we hope it is the ambulance, the police, anyone to come and help us. I look out the window, and Father John and Sister Mary Margaret get out of their car. Two other nuns have come to help. They look at all the damage round them, then Sister Mary Margaret sees me. She's awful mad, so mad that her mouth is moving afore her words can come out.

"Robert, come here." I go and tell her that Miss Alice is all beat up. She sends the two nuns in to help Mama with Miss Alice.

"Well, Father?"

"Yes. Sister you were right. 'Tis even worse than I ever dreamed possible."

"Words won't help right now, Father," Sister snaps. She reaches into the car and brings out boxes of sandwiches, hands them to me, and orders me to put them on the hood of the car. She brings out a big blue thermos of coffee and paper cups. All the neighbors begin to come to the car. She nods to the coffee and some begin to pour it out.

"Robert. It is time to get to work." She snaps open a garbage bag, and it sounds like a gunshot. She stomps over to begin to pick up the trash that the strangers had thrown round in the night. "Come on, Father, you too. You can pray while you work." So Father gets a bag and goes across the street to pick up stuff there.

"Were you afraid, Robert?" Sister asks me as we start to fill the trash bag.

"I was scared, but now I'm mad."

"The Good Lord knows that I don't believe in anger. But at a time like this, you will need a tough emotion like anger to make you stronger." Sister looks up and sees the Guffman's trailer. "Holy Mother of God," she says as she crosses herself. Her strong black shoes cover the distance from where we are to the Guffman's trailer in a second. She stares at it, and words I never would believe a nun knew are whispered under her breath.

"What are we standing here for?" she demands. "Bib, go into the car and take out the cleanser from the back seat and all the rags."

I do as she says. She grabs it from me and uses a bucket of water that Mr. Guffman had filled. Soon, we all join her, and I don't know if it was the cleanser or Sister's temper, but the red and black paint begin to get fainter and fainter. Sister looks at Mrs. Guffman, who isn't crying so hard now.

"We are washing away evil."

127

"We are washing away evil," Mrs. Guffman repeats.

An ambulance drives slowly to Miss Alice's door, and soon, she's being carried out on a stretcher. Mama is crying and holding Miss Alice's hand. The ambulance men won't let Mama go with. When it drives away, I go to her and Daddy drives up with Mr. Johnson.

"How is she?" Mr. Johnson asks.

"I don't know." Mama is still crying.

"I'm going to follow them to the hospital." Mr. Johnson turns his Ford round and follows the ambulance.

"Where are the police, Sam? Didn't you go to the police?"

"Yes, we notified the police."

"Well? Where are they?"

"They will be here, Claire. When they're ready, they will come."

CHAPTER SIXTEEN

All this month—March, that is—Miss Alice has been in the hospital. Every morning, Mama takes two buses to get to the Ramsey County Hospital in St. Paul. Daddy's worried 'coz Mama's tummy is getting bigger, and he says she needs more rest. But Mama's like a lady possessed. She can't let a day go by without visiting. She said that I can't go see Miss Alice until she's better. I miss her a lot, and I write letters and draw pictures to send, and I let her know how Cannon Weight and Tom are doing. Mama puts the letters in her straw basket where there are grapes or peaches waiting for Miss Alice to eat and, maybe, a magazine to look at. Books are too heavy, Mama says. She says the hospital food is terrible and not enough to feed a sparrow.

The only good thing that came out about all this is Dill gets to stay with me and sleeps in my own bed. When I get home from school, Dill yawns and sits up while I tell him about my day. Then we both go over and take care of the other pets, and I pick up round the trailer some. Miss Alice gave me my very own key to her brand-new front door after Daddy put it in. I wear it round my neck on a piece of blue yarn and don't even take it off when I shower so's I don't lose it.

After all the yards and trailers were messed up, the police came but didn't have much in the way of help to offer. They walked round some and asked questions, wrote a bit down, and then just left. I don't reckon that was much of a vestigation. Daddy was gonna go to the station house to see someone he says is higher in authority, but Mama told him to let it be for now. Daddy didn't agree much with Mama, you could tell 'coz he pressed his lips together. But he didn't say nothing. He don't want to upset Mama more than she already is, what with the baby and all.

Felicity took down the striped Indian blanket in our room and pushed our beds together close, so we're almost in the same bed. We all go to bed together now, I mean at the same time, and we leave our bedroom doors open. Even though it's still cold outside, Daddy banks the fire in the stove at night and double locks the door. We used to have just a dirty old chain on the door, but above that is a shiny brass bolt now. I like to look at it; it makes me feel safer.

No one's been able to get in touch with the landlord, Mr. Alderson. He's been up north in Duluth ice fishing for the past week. Daddy says Mr. Alderson is on a "convenient vacation." I had to think on those words a while. I reckon this: Daddy thinks Mr. Alderson has something to do with all that went on round here. I can't hardly believe it. I remember how Jimmy and I used to practice with our slangshots shooting cans offa his fence. Mr. Alderson is a real sharp shoot with a slangshot.

Anyway, it's been more than four weeks since it happened, all the yards are pretty well cleared out and the ugly marks on the Guffman's trailer are gone. Widder Alva is leaving today to go and live with her daughter in Little Falls. She's too scared to stay here anymore. Widder Alva done told me nothing like this has ever happened before and it's all 'coz of that awful music that America got from England. She says this new music turns young people into savages. Daddy talked with her serious like to make sure she was making the decision she really wants to make. Mama jumped right in and told her to go. Mama has a real good sense of trouble. She always had that, and the way she acts makes me afeared of what might come next. She won't let Felicity or me out of her sight. We get up, go to school, come home, do our homework, do something else like watch television or play with Dill, go to bed. That's all. Daddy's trying to work another extra shift now and again. He stays up and watches out the window sometimes until Mama makes him come to bed. Mama's taken to scolding Daddy just like one of us kids.

Today is Saturday, the last Saturday in March, and Mama is letting me go to the hospital with her. We wait in the cold at the bus stop, me asking lots of questions Mama doesn't seem to hear. When we get uptown, the bus lets us off on Main Street in front of Rind's Drug Store. This bus goes on to Minneapolis, so we have to get off and wait for the one that goes to St. Paul. Mama says we just have to wait when I ask her why we need to get another bus and how long it will take and if the hospital is a far walk. That's not really an answer, but I keep that to myself.

Mr. Rind runs the drug store along with his wife and his oldest son. He put little tables and chairs along the front window, and you can get a soda or cup of coffee if it's too cold to wait for the bus sitting on our green bench outside.

I like to come to the drugstore, usually to look at comic books, and sometimes to drink a soda. Mr. Rind is always nice to us, and now, Mrs. Rind is on her way over, clucking like a little hen. She puts a hand on Mama's back and asks her how she is. Mama doesn't talk as much as she usually does to people, and I can't help staring at her, wondering. Mama's always been so friendly. "Smiles are free," she used to say and she liked to give her smile out to everyone we meet. It is a beautiful smile.

Mrs. Rind comes back with Mama's coffee and my Coke. Mama pays her, so she don't have to bother with change if the bus comes. She puts down a dime on the table for a tip. I reckon the dime is her smile today.

"Mama, can we change seats?"

"Why?"

"I just don't want to look out the window." I sip my Coke, making bubbles at the bottom of the glass.

"I've told you a hundred times not to blow down your straw. I thought you liked to look out the window to see the bus coming."

"Not this window. Please? Can we change?"

Mama gets up, gathers her things, and waits for me to change seats. I'm glad she doesn't press it, 'coz I don't want to tell her I don't want to look across the street at Dr. Dailey's dental office. It gives me the creeps. I swear, I can hear the drill from here. Daddy says Dr. Dailey is a fine dentist, but I think he's mean and likes to hurt people. Maybe he escaped from prison just to set up office here in Crystal Springs so he can be mean and get paid for it too. To my way of thinking, anyone who would want to be a dentist must be touched in the head. I don't trust dentists at all.

Mark Rind, the druggist's son, comes over to visit. He does the sweeping in the store and stocks the shelves. Even though Mark is twenty-two, he can't read. His daddy showed him how to stock the shelves going by color and sizes. He picked it up fast, just like everything else he does. Sometimes, kids like to hang outside the window and make fun of him. Mark knows I'd never do that, and he gives me a piece of bubble gum, the kind that has little comic strips in them. Mama makes me put it in my pocket for later because the bus is going to come soon, and I might choke on it during the ride.

The bus is real crowded when we get on, and there isn't a seat left. Daddy always told me that a gentleman gives his seat up for a lady, but here are all sorts of men, looking ahead and ignoring Mama as she sways her big tummy back and forth while hanging onto a strap. I'm not big enough to reach the leather straps overhead, so I'm holding onto a metal pole all slippery from the hands that have held it afore me. The bus hits a hole in the road, and I accidentally let go, falling into a seat on top of a woman holding some knitting in her lap.

"Careful," says the woman, pulling away from me. Mama looks round, but I just smile and apologize and take my place again at the pole. After three stops, the bus empties out some, and I find a seat for both of us. I lean on Mama and fall asleep. When she wakes me up at our stop, I feel more awake than I've done for a long time. I skip down the road, watching out for mailboxes and hydrants all the while. One time, I walked smack into a mailbox and knocked myself down. It was all because I wasn't looking where I was going. This is one of Felicity's favorite stories, and she tells it a lot, mostly to embarrass me.

At the hospital, we take the elevator to the third floor. Mama asks at the desk how Miss Alice is. Her voice is hushed so I don't hear. We walk down the hall, and though I try not to, I look into the rooms that have their doors open. There seems to be an awful lot of sick people packed in each room on this floor. One man is lying, all shrunk into his bedclothes. He's got a clear tube round his mouth and stuck up his nose. His eyes look into mine, and I feel like he wants something from me that I can't give him. I stand there, looking back at him, one hand on the door to hold me up. I almost feel dizzy, looking into those eyes that are like magnets. Then the old man looks away, out the window, outside where I think he's never going again.

"Come along, Bib," Mama calls to me softly by another door. I go in, and Miss Alice is sitting up in bed, smiling at me. I run, forgetting that I'm not sposed to, and throw my arms round her.

"Careful," Miss Alice says, a lot nicer than the woman on the bus. It's awful strange how the same word can sound so different. Miss Alice kisses me, and I stand back to get a good look at her. Her head is all bandaged, but the bruises on her face are almost gone, no more black, just a yellowish gold color. One of her arms is in a cast, and I get to sign my name with a pen she hands me.

"When you comin' home, Miss Alice?"

"Tuesday, April the second. Why, do you miss me?" Mama hands her some green grapes, and she starts eating them.

"Course I do. And so do Cannon Weight, Tom and Dill. Look." I show her the house key that hangs round my neck. I'm real proud that I haven't lost it. She gives me a one arm hug, then we settle down for some talk. There are three other women crowded in the room, the beds are so close together you hafta draw a thin cloth curtain to feel alone while you talk. The other women don't have visitors, so Mama draws the curtain some and goes over to talk with them.

"How is it here?" I'm awful curious. I've never been in a hospital afore, never even had my tonsils out like Jimmy and Simon Peter done.

"Awful, Bib. Just awful. Light on all night, when you're trying to sleep, dim bulbs on all day when you're trying to read. And the food! Heavens above! I haven't tasted such disgusting food since the one and only time I spent Thanksgiving dinner with my sister Caroline. I asked her, you know, if she'd want me to bring anything, but you know how stubborn she is, Bib."

"Yes, ma'am."

"Stubborn as the day is long, and a worse cook you never would meet. I think she's cooking for this hospital now, and too ashamed to tell me. Which she should be if that ever happened, everyone knowing hospital food is tasteless mush."

"Yes, ma'am." I'm so glad to hear her, she sounds as good as normal.

"Jello, morning, noon and night. It's all the same, jello, jello, jello. And flat ginger ale. Don't they have a refrigerator anywhere in this huge building?"

"I love jello," I tell her.

Miss Alice smiles at me, reaches round and gives me a small plastic cup with jello cubes in it. Lime, my favorite.

CHAPTER SEVENTEEN

After school today, Felicity, Mama, and me are going to the church for a celebration. It's the Feast of Saint Benedict the Black, April 4, and Father John has planned a party. Mama was surprised at this; she said she never saw the like. But Father John told her he'd always had a fondness for this St. Benedict. He's patron saint of the colored people, being he was a Negro slave that was let go and became very holy. At school, Sister tells us the story of his life and talks some about how the colored people are still being treated bad, especially down south. And sometimes in the north too, but I guess not as much. I could swear she was looking at Jimmy when she said this, but maybe not.

Mama told Daddy to meet us at the church after work. Daddy laughed and said leave it to Father John. He loves a celebration, and if he can teach a lesson at the same time, Father is even happier.

Sometimes, I have Father John teach me at school. He wanders in the class and leads us in prayers or asks us questions. I guess when he got to be a priest he didn't get to teach no more, so now he likes to take over once on a while.

The church has a small recreation hall in the basement. It's got old folding chairs round a little old tables, a crucifix on the wall and an old piano that's missing some of the keys. Even though it's missing keys, Widder Alva could get some good tunes out of that piano, but tonight she can't 'coz she done moved away.

The tables are covered with pretty blue cloths and candles are flickering in the middle of them. There's a big punch bowl and paper plates of any type of bar you could want, chocolate, peanut butter, and coconut too. Big shiny urns of coffee for the grownups are on either side; they look like big metal bookends. There's also heating plates of all kinds of hot dish and vegetables. An ice chest holds cans of soda for the kids. Seems to me, everything you could want to eat is on that table, and it makes me mighty hungry.

All the neighbors from the trailer park are there, even the Guffmans who don't go to this church 'coz they like to pray at home. I can see some of the town people too, even Protestants are invited and some came. Over to the side, I spy Jimmy and his parents. Jimmy lets out a whoop and runs round some people to get to me.

"Where's your mom?" I ask, all nervous.

"Never mind," says Jimmy. "She says I can play with you all I want."

"What made her change her mind?"

"Dunno. Who cares? Look at how shiny the floor is over there. Let's take off our shoes and slide."

"Okay."

We do, and we have a great old time until our mamas come over, catch our ears, and make us stop. So we go over to the food table and get punch and a plate of cookies and bars. No one pays enough attention to us to tell us we'll spoil our suppers; they're too busy talking to each other. We pile our plates high and hide in the back to eat.

Father John walks over to the podium and starts to talk. No one hears him because the microphone isn't on. Sister Mary Margaret goes over and looks at the microphone. You'd think it'd start right there and then, the way she looked at it, but it didn't. Then a man from the crowd fixes it, and the high squeal it makes is a terrifying, squeaky sound and we all cover our ears.

"I'm truly sorry about that," Father says. Some laughter rises and floats round Father's face. "Dear friends, we have come together to celebrate the life of a very blessed saint, surely 'tis one of me favorites. But afore I begin, I've been asked by Alice Betchelder, dear woman, to thank you for your gifts and especially your prayers. She can't be with us tonight, poor soul, but she'll be up and about soon."

All the people applaud. Miss Alice has been home for two days, and she told me she never felt so strong afore, not since she headlocked her sister Caroline, after her sister Caroline took away Miss Alice's boyfriend.

"'Twould be no lie in me tellin' you I had hoped more of our townspeople would be with us this night. Trouble has come to our town, as we know only too well, and together, we must stand in the Body of Christ to show our love and support of each other." Father takes out a handkerchief and wipes his forehead. He makes a movement with his hand to let us know we can sit down. "Now, a story I'll be tellin' you, and a truer story you will never hear. Sure, and I wouldn't be standin' here if 'tweren't true. So. On a Saturday, when I was a lad back in Ireland, I used to go fishin' in the creek down the ways by an old stone wall. That wall was covered with wild roses, of the like you'll never see anywhere else. The colors! Ah, well, I was tellin' that while I was fishin' I heard a group of lads walkin' down the lane. One of them, me mate Peter, who I write to even to this day, called to me askin' and how the fish be bitin'. I jumped the wall because I was younger then, and we started to talk together. A glorious Saturday it was. Not a drop of rain if you can believe me. And of a sudden, one lad asked Peter 'And why be you talkin' to him, and him being a Catholic?' Peter, you see, was Protestant. So were his friends. As were many more people in the village where I was born. And Peter, not knowin' how to be a man, lad that he was, turned his back on me and with his friends walked away down the lane."

Father paused then, looking at the faces looking back at him. I could see in my mind that little boy who was so hurt by his friend, all because they went to different churches.

"And so it 'twas, my friends, and so 'tis today. One people hating another. Fighting and the blood shed staining the beautiful green of Ireland. Today is the Feast Day of St. Benedict the Black. Let us be rememberin' this holy man, a slave freed by his master, taunted by his fellow men back in sixteenth century Sicily because of the color of his skin. He was a Negro to be sure, black as the night and a more kind and holy than any one of us can ever hope to be. Do you be thinkin' this, and let us gather together and love one another."

Father steps back from the microphone. No one says a word; some people seem to be finding their shoes very interesting. Mama wipes a tear from her eye then. 'Coz she likes to be busy, she goes over to help at the food table.

Now Father is moving in and out of the crowd of people, making them laugh and sometimes picking up a child for a hug. A few people leave by the side door, trying to sneak out, and I don't think they've even eaten any bars or cookies. Jimmy and I go back for seconds; the thinning crowd leaves more for us. I put a coconut bar in my pocket when no one looks, to take back to Dill. He loves to chew on coconut, even when it gets stuck in his teeth, and he's gotta shake his head and paw at his teeth and ears.

We're having so much fun that no one notices the time. Mrs. Baker serves up hotdish at the table and huge fresh buns and the like. We eat and visit some more. One of the ladies from the choir plays the piano; she's none too good, hitting a lot of sour notes and all. No one really cares. We sing songs, and Father sings some of his Irish songs that make him cry.

I look up, and Daddy is standing at the platform, his seed cap in his dirty hands and his eyes sad and tearful. Mama goes to him. The room becomes oddly quiet and Father joins Mama and Daddy. Daddy tells them something, and Mama clings to him. I see Father finger the big iron cross he always wears, then he crosses hisself, and goes to the microphone.

We are all quiet. We are all waiting.

"Friends." Father's voice shakes with tears, and he clears his throat to try again. "Friends, a black day has come upon us. We have just heard that Dr. Martin Luther King, Jr. has been shot."

The quiet is suffocating.

Father John deepens his voice. "God rest his soul."

"God rest his soul," we echo.

"Let us pray."

In one body, we kneel right there on the floor of the hall.

"O God, who dost always pity and spare, we humbly beseech Thee for the soul of Thy servant Dr. Martin Luther King, Jr."

CHAPTER EIGHTEEN

Last night and this morning, we all knelt and told the rosary for Mr. King and his family. School was called out, and Daddy took the day off work, even without pay.

Mama sits with empty eyes as the face of Mr. King rolls over and over the television screen. He seemed such a nice man, and when he spoke about freedom and such it sure put shivers up and down my back. His family is so sad.

The television has been on all day, and none of us has gone out. Miss Alice came over with Dill and watched the news program. It is a strange silence in this room that was so happy such a little while ago. Mrs. Guffman came over with a basket of sandwiches, and Daddy made coffee. It was like everyone was hypnotized by that screen; we couldn't keep our eyes off of it. Felicity left and I could hear her lock our bedroom door.

Once on a while, other people were talking on the news, white people and black folks, offering sympathy to the family and to the country. Some of them seemed to mean what they said, and some didn't. I don't understand why. Mr. King was done shot dead, just like Uncle Simon, and there are a few people saying he done deserved what came to him. I asked Daddy what they meant, but he didn't answer me. To my way of thinking, there's nothing a person says or does that deserves to be shot dead.

"A hope has died," says Miss Alice to me. And that's all she said.

I go outside to sit on the step with Dill. He's playing with a dried leaf that's been set free by the melted snow. First he chases it, pounces on it, looks at it, and sits back until the leaf flies of again. It's one of his favorite games, only trouble is I can't join in. I tried once, but he got disgusted and walked off. I reckon it's a cat game not a people game.

Suddenly, I hear Mama call me in and told me to stay inside and not go out. Daddy is on the phone with Mr. Selter, he's worried about something, and I can tell it's bad. I look at the television and see crowds and crowds of angry people, hitting and hurting each other and yelling names of all kinds. Miss Alice shuts the TV off and the quiet is heavy as Daddy speaks.

"Can't tell you how much I appreciate you letting me know, Willy...Yes. Yes, Father John called and the women and children will go over to the church...I understand...No, I think the best thing for you is to stay at home. If there's any real trouble, I'll get word to you. Under other circumstances, I would agree with you, but I believe that today, we will be shut off from police protection...Thank you for calling them." Then Daddy laughs, not a daddy laugh, but kinda crazy-like.

"Yes, Willy, we know our rights…The problem comes from the few who don't believe in those rights…I must go now. Many thanks for all you've done…Yes, I'll keep in touch."

He hangs up the phone slowly, and it takes him a long while to turn round. Mama is staring at him, her eyes big and shiny like mirrors. Miss Alice is supporting her with her good arm.

"What is it, Sam?"

"There's a rumor of a mob rising in town."

"Only a rumor?" I can tell Mama doesn't want it to be true.

"A rumor with validity, I would say. Willy Selter spoke with Mr. Johnson and some others here at the park. Father John wants all of the women and children to go to the church."

Mama starts crying like I've never heard afore. Like a wild animal. It scares me. Daddy goes over to her then, his arms round her, stroking her hair. "Claire, Claire, please. It's only for this night and only as a precaution."

"I won't leave you."

"You must. You must take the children and go. Miss Alice, you might want to go home and pack a few things." She nods and goes out the door and across the dirt road that's all muddy. Her shoes sink in the mud and as I watch from the open door, I can hear them making sucking noises as she walks. Dill complains about the mud all the way home.

Daddy tells me to sit quietly and read while he takes Mama into their bedroom to rest a while. I try and read but can't. I go and knock on the bedroom door, and after a while, Felicity opens the door, and I crawl into bed with her.

When I wake up, the room is in shadows. Felicity is gone, and I can hear her and Mama getting supper ready. I go out to the kitchen, and we all help to put supper on. None of us is very hungry so we have leftovers heated up on the stove and canned peaches for dessert. When Mama does take a bite of food, her hand shakes so that you can hear her teeth hit the metal of the fork.

In the distance, I think I hear what sounds like a roar. Not loud like a lion, but something creeping, creeping through the night. We all stop eating to listen. Doors are opening and closing round us, the neighbors are getting together in the road waiting to meet what is coming.

Felicity wants to be brave. She wants to be brave for Mama and me, but she don't know how. She says, "Well, anyway, what I think we should do is just move away. Like Widow Alva. We can find an apartment in St. Cloud. Father can find a job easily there. There are more opportunities in a big city. I hate this old tin can we live in anyway. That's all it is, it's all it'll ever be. Everyone thinks we're common, only common trash live in tin cans like these." She stops, and her face shows that she knows she's done gone too far.

Daddy stands up at the table. "No," he says and even though his voice is quiet and slow, it's real firm and a more honest sound I never heard. "No. These trailers are not tin cans packed with common folk, Felicity. These are homes. They are our homes. Homes we work for, and sweat for and thank the Lord for each day we step in the dooryard after spending one hell of a long day picking over potatoes on a conveyor belt. This is a home that your mother keeps safe for us, cleans and sews curtains for, and fills with the richness of her love. Yes, and more than that. These are our chariots, the chariots of the poor warriors armed only with the strength of the work left in our bodies. Strength is our weapon and work is our virtue, and no one can ever take that away from us. You children are young, too young to learn what you will have to learn tonight. Sometimes, in this whole big wide world, there is only a little bit of space you can call your own. It is true that the landlord calls all the shots, and he collects his pound of flesh every month, most times without keeping any promises. He can raise the rent. He controls that little part of you. But you pay, and for that month, it is yours. You pay in good faith that this home will be standing for you to live in, to protect your family from the evil outside. And now this evil is coming here, involving all of us. And it's a big evil." His eyes are bright and his hands shake as he clutches the edge of the table. "Yes, it's big and it's ugly and it's an evil that has hurt millions of people the world over since Cain killed Abel. But we won't let it get to us."

Daddy looks tall and terrible under that light. Mama asks him once more not to go. He lifts her up, and they look at each other for a long time. He gives her a happy smile and shakes his head.

"Sister is waiting for you. Take the children and go to her."

"I won't let you go!"

"Claire. Would you have me hide?"

Mama looks at him a long moment. "No. No, Sam, you are right. I know you have to go."

"Take the children to the church. We must protect our own."

Mama nods. Daddy reaches for his seed cap that hangs on its own nail next to the stove so it will stay warmed up. He doesn't look back as he leaves.

We watch him walk right through the circle of light that shines over our door into the darkness beyond.

CHAPTER NINETEEN

Mama hurried us along, finding blankets and pillows and such to keep us warm. We meet the neighbors in the middle of the street, all the women and their children wrapped up against the cold night air.

"Where is Miss Alice?" someone asks. We get worried and go to her door. Mama calls her name, and Miss Alice opens it.

"I'm not running away, Claire."

"Alice, you just got out of the hospital. You must come with us."

"I'm not leaving my home. They can come do what they will. I may not be young enough to fight for a cause, but I'm damn sure I'm old enough to die for one."

I can hear Cannon Weight whining inside, but the trailer ain't lit, and I can't see nothing. The women are arguing: some want to leave Miss Alice to her foolishness, some want to force her to go with us. Behind her yard, I can see figures beyond the cornfield; the Sisters are waiting for us to bring us to shelter. Then I look along to the end of the dirt road where the men have gone, and I can see a mob of people moving fast down the main road. Some are yelling some are carrying things like torches of fire to light their way.

"Mama." I point to the mob of people. Mama rattles the door again and calls to Miss Alice.

"Go away!" is all we hear.

The woman and children have moved ahead of us and are creeping along the cornfield trying to be quiet. Some of the children are scared and crying. Felicity takes Mama's arm and my hand and forces us to walk faster. The cornfield is full of mud, it's mighty hard going, but we soon reach the other side.

"This way," says Mother Mary Robert. She's holding a big red flashlight and leads us along the path to the church. It's rocky and some of us stumble a little as we go down an incline. Mama almost falls, and I get afeared for the baby inside her.

We reach the basement steps of the church, but instead of going into the hall, she leads us up the stairs, behind the choir section and into the pews.

"Lay your blankets on these," Mother says, taking a baby in her arms to give Mrs. Wright a rest. "I will bring you more blankets and the Sisters will bring food and coffee. This is a time when the Lord will be thankful that his people are eating and sleeping in the shelter of His home. You will be safe here." She lays the baby down gently onto a cushion of blanket. Her long skirts swish as she moves quickly away.

Mama drops on her knees and begins to pray quietly. I look at the red-lighted lamp that shows us Jesus and present. I'm not kneeling. I'm not praying. I'm wondering where He is. I'm asking Him why. Why do we have to go through all this, just 'coz we want to live a life as normal as Jimmy and his family. Mama's hands are clenched, and she is being faithful, but my heart does not fill with love. I rebel 'coz I'm too damn mad.

From where we are, we can't see nothing that is going on in the street. Mother Mary Robert comes back and some of the Sisters to make us more comfortable in the pews. Children are falling asleep, and Felicity sits like a piece of wood, staring at nothing and looking almost fragile.

Mother begins a prayer for our safekeeping, and others take it up, it's like one soft voice begging God for mercy, for safety. I ask Mama where His mercy is right now, but she doesn't hear me. Sister Mary Margaret comes to me and tries to hold me. I push her away and run to the very back of the church.

"Let him go." I hear Sister tell Mama. "He needs time alone, time to think."

What I'm thinking of, it's Daddy and Old Mr. Johnson. And there's Mr. Guffman who has already met with so much evil in his life. All the other men standing alone at the end of that muddy road. And I think of Miss Alice, her kindness, how she's like another mama to me. How she never yells or cares about how I might act or what I might think. About Dill, Tom, and Cannon Weight. I decide right then to go back.

I wait for another prayer to start; voices are becoming a little louder in strength as they pray to God. I sneak over to the side door. The crossbar is cold in my hand, and I push it gently so it doesn't make a sound. I slip outside and close the door as quiet as I can.

Then I run.

I must have fallen a hundred times, and it must have taken me a hundred years to cross that cornfield and get to Miss Alice's backyard. I run down the street and hide behind the front edge of Mr. Johnson's trailer so I can see what's going on.

Daddy and the other men are still waiting at the foot of the road. Some of the men have shovels and clubs with them. Daddy has nothing. Under the streetlight, his black face is calm and not angry at all. He is standing there, just standing there and watching the crowd of meanness come to meet him. Daddy always believed men could discuss both sides of a problem and there would be a solution that could make everyone happy. I think of this, but I don't believe it. There is too much badness in the faces of that crowd.

"We want no nigras here! We want no nigras here!"

"Nigra trash, get out!"

"Jews go back to where you came from! No nigras, no Jews!"

They are surrounding my daddy and clubs are swinging, fists are hitting, feet are kicking. Then an awful groaning sound as a man in a red shirt hits someone with a club and he falls down. I see the face of the man who fell. Two men pass by me, don't see me, and go on down to Miss Alice's trailer. They scream outside the door, pull on the door, but Daddy's good lock holds them out.

Then one of them pours something along the ground next to the trailer and another one puts his torch of fire down to feed it. A line of fire starts, right in front of her door. The flames come alive and lick up the side of her house.

I run to her. I go along the back and bang on that door. I don't care if anyone hears me; I've lost all sense except to help Miss Alice and her animals. She opens the door and stumbles out into the yard. While she's lying there, trying to catch her breath, I see Mama come running to help and pull her away from the danger of the flames. Afore she can see me, I run inside. Cannon Weight rushes out of the door, followed by Tom. But I can't see Dill anywhere.

I start to call him; Mama hears me and yells for me to get out. By now, the fire is all round the trailer, and the air is filled with an awful thick smoke. It hurts my eyes and my nose, and my throat is so raw I can hardly breathe. I go down the hallway and push open Miss Alice's bedroom door, and I find Dill, sound asleep on a pillow. I grab him and rush to the door. The fire is a live thing, waiting for me. Through it I can see Mama and Felicity is holding her back from coming into where I am. I feel a great tiredness like I never done felt afore, and heavy, so heavy. Overhead the crackling sound is loud and something falls and hits me on the head. I throw Dill through an opening in the flames and try to see if he lands all right. Then I go to sleep.

CHAPTER TWENTY

When I open my eyes, I'm on a nice cool patch of grass. There's no more fire-bright light to hurt my eyes. The smoke is drifting away from me, but it's all over me just the same. Someone has put a blanket on me, I wanna scream to take it off 'coz it's so heavy and I never did feel so much pain in all my life. I can't open my mouth to tell 'em. I can't even move.

"Bib, Bib." Mama is sobbing next to me, afeared that touching me will hurt me. One arm is cradling her tummy to protect my baby brother inside. Like Daddy said tonight, to protect our own.

I think of the face of the man who fell first. And I remember it was Daddy. My Daddy is dead, and I'll never see him again. I'm hoping right now, he's up in heaven and my other daddy is shaking his hand and telling him what a fine man Daddy is, and thank you for loving my son.

There's a lot of wetness on my cheeks, and it's tears from the pain and the smoke. I can't stop 'em. When I try and close my eyes, Mama sobs louder than ever, so I open them again so's she won't think I'm dead.

One of the white men, the one in the red shirt who carried a club comes over to us.

"Ma'am, an ambulance will be coming soon."

Mama snarls at him like a mad dog and turns away.

This man, he steps back away from her. He's afraid when he looks down at me, and I can't figger out why. He sure looks different than he did when he was swinging that club and screaming those ugly names. Now I notice how still they all are, hanging round us in a wide, wide circle. Some other people are crying, women but men too. It sounds like a sad song—a song I don't want to go to sleep by.

Off in the distance, I hear sirens coming closer, and I'm sure hoping this pain will stop soon. I try and think the pain away. I think of Daddy and how proud he looked when he called us poor warriors at the supper table.

Daddy and me. We're warriors, and our chariot is still there, reflecting the dying fire that used to be Miss Alice's trailer.

A soft sound rushes at me as I'm lying on the grass. It's Dill. He reaches up a paw to touch my face and begins to lick the tears away as the sirens become louder.